James was born and bred in Liverpool, UK, but has been teaching in a small international school in Hong Kong for the last 18 years. His book is very loosely based on his experiences there. It is a humorous story which contains slightly bonkers teachers, students and parents of a fictional school located right on a beach.

He lives in Hong Kong with his wife, Suzy; daughter, Ellie; son, Joe; and long-haired guinea pig called George.

JAMES LAMBERT

THE ALMOST TRUE STORY of SANDY PRIMARY SCHOOL

Hope you enjoy!

Jim Lambert

AUSTIN MACAULEY PUBLISHERS™

LONDON ∗ CAMBRIDGE ∗ NEW YORK ∗ SHARJAH

Copyright © James Lambert (2019)

A CIP catalogue record for this title is available from the British Library.

ISBN 9781528910019 (Paperback)
ISBN 9781528910026 (Kindle e-book)
ISBN 9781528959452 (ePub e-book)

www.austinmacauley.com

First Published (2019)
Austin Macauley Publishers Ltd
25 Canada Square
Canary Wharf
London
E14 5LQ

For Suzy, Ellie, Joe and all the teachers, parents and students – past and present – of the best little school in Hong Kong.

CONTENTS

THE REBUILD

"Well, thank you all for coming here today, please take a seat."

The children looked at each other quizzically, then stared blankly at Mr Bell. They were all standing on a beautiful beach covered in pristine white sand. Mr Bell had his back to the ocean, facing the children and facing the blazing sun which was reflecting off his sunglasses and making his salt and pepper hair glint.

"On the sand?" inquired Jack.

"Yes, yes, on the sand, chop, chop!" Mr Bell replied while gesturing his hands to sit.

The children pulled up a shell.

"Now, I know you have all been extremely busy these last couple of months, probably creating wondrous worlds in Minecraft or watching the exciting lives of these insightful YouTube stars," the sarcasm was dripping from Mr Bell's voice. "But I have gathered you here today to impart to you some exceptionally exciting news!"

There was a babble of inaudible groans and mutters, there was also a growing realisation of what this exciting news could be. The children, around twenty of them, shifted uncomfortably, they were away from the safety of their cyber-worlds and a huge dose of reality was about to hit home.

Ellie looked up from her book, "I bet you the school is reopening," she whispered to no one in particular.

"The school is reopening!" announced Mr Bell cheerfully.

"I knew it," whispered Ellie to no one in particular and went back to her book.

More groans and mutterings.

"Now, come on, I know you don't mean it."

Even more groans and mutterings.

"But that's not the exciting news, that's the brilliant news," Mr Bell spoke in a slightly raised teacher tone in an attempt to bring a bit of order to his sandy squad. "We all knew the school would eventually reopen, but the really exciting news is that…"

"Why did the school close again?" enquired Bob.

"Hurricane Bob!" The children and teacher all chorused together.

"That should have been the Hurricane comma Bob," corrected Tim, "The Hurricane was actually called Hurricane Soft and Fluffy after the meteorologists who first spotted it, Dr Soft and Professor Fluffy."

"That's right Tim, I am sure Bob does remember that a couple of months ago, the school was completely destroyed by a category 10 Hurricane; Hurricane Soft and Fluffy," Mr Bell took a sip of tea from his reusable plastic cup and chuckled to himself, "Ironic, I know."

"Awesome!" cried Bob.

"No, not awesome Bob, devastating, everything was destroyed, everything was lost…luckily it struck at 3.05 pm so all the staff and kids were well gone, so no one got hurt."

The children nodded in unison that indeed they had had a lucky escape but then Kyle piped up, "That's not quite true Mr Bell, what about Mr Grimshaw? He got very hurt, like dead hurt, that's what my mum said."

"We don't know that for sure Kyle," Mr Bell replied looking slightly uncomfortable at the way the conversation was going.

"My mum told me that the police found his tattered underwear, up a tree about three miles from here," Kyle retorted as he gestured to the woodland that lay beyond the beach.

"Definitely dead," said Oscar.

"How did the police know that the undies belonged to Mr Grimshaw?" inquired Bob, who as usual was one step behind with events.

"They were clearly labelled, that's what my mum said, it was all over Facebook and Twitter," Kyle announced confidently, whilst standing up and facing the rest of the children, like he was breaking the latest news on TV.

Mr Bell, clearly exasperated by how his meeting had been hijacked by Kyle and his font of all knowledge—his mum—tried to get things back on track, "Look I know in certain areas, like Facetube and Youbook, it was common knowledge that Mr Grimshaw labelled his undergarments, but that doesn't mean that he actually died," he took another sip of tea and continued, "Anyway between us, Mr Dijon, the school owner was going to fire him anyway, his y-fronts may have been in tip-top order, but sadly his classroom wasn't."

Kyle opened his mouth and Mr Bell shot him a glance, as if to say, if you mention your mum and underwear in the same sentence again, then the story of the boy buried head-first in the sand by an angry teacher would soon go viral.

"So..." a slightly calmer Mr Bell continued after taking a huge breath, "The incredibly exciting news is that Mr Dijon, along with your Principal Mr X, had a meeting with some very powerful government men from the Education Department, and after a six-hour lunch meeting on Mr Dijon's yacht, you will never guess what they have decided?"

Now, it's always a mistake to ask a group of ten year olds to guess something, as the assumption is that most of them are actually listening to what is being said and that the answers could be in some way relevant.

After a free-for-all shouting session, Mr Bell summarised their ideas, "No, not free hover cars for all children, nor a pet lizard for anyone named Jack, free cucumbers for all pet moles, or a year's supply of ice-cream or even introducing an extra month in the year between May and June called Colin. These are all marvellous ideas children but let's get back to why we are here today."

Shrugs from the children as if to indicate their ideas were all valid and they looked a little surprised that they hadn't actually guessed the correct answer.

"The exciting news is that the government people will not only fund a rebuild of our school but they want you to design it and decide where it should be located!"

Silence. Absolute silence.

"So, the government want us, your class of poor likkle orphans to design a school, decide where it goes and make all the decisions, cor blimey govna'?" Hettie asked dramatically while putting her hands on her lapels.

"As we have talked about many times Hettie, none of you are poor orphans and for the final time, you are not from the Victorian age, but yes essentially that's the plan."

"Erm...why?" the kids all asked together.

"Because you guys are amazing and the government think your ideas will be stunning."

There was a chorus of, "Really?"

None of the children were truly convinced. "Look, never look a gift horse in the mouth," said Mr Bell.

"Do we get a free horse with the new school?" asked Bob. "If so, can I have a grey one?"

"No Bob, it's a phrase meaning don't turn away a once in a lifetime opportunity."

"I know that story, it's about the wooden horse, don't they also say beware of Geeks bringing gifts," blurted Dave.

"It's Greeks Dave, not Geeks," Tim muttered, clearly annoyed by his friend's lack of historical knowledge.

"We aren't in Greece, and you can always trust the government," Mr Bell said lying through his teeth (about the government that is, they weren't in Greece, that bit was true).

The children looked at each other and started muttering that maybe this was a great chance to make a difference and Mr Bell took his opportunity.

"History tells us that adults tend to only think about money, children's minds are pure and honest, and for once, the government wants to be proud of a project, hand it over to the people who are going to be affected by the decisions the most, give the children the ownership of their own future, give you fine young people, the ownership of your own futures," said Mr Bell who had subconsciously been making a pile of sand under his feet since the meeting began, and now he stood on top of it, commanding respect. There were a couple of gulps from the children, Lucy was actually crying and there was a real sense that for once, adults, particularly those in power were prepared to do the right thing.

"Besides," said Mr Bell, "Whatever happens, the government are planning to sell the story to Hollywood and make a tonne of money."

The children decided to gloss over the last piece of information, and nodded their heads in approval.

From his sandy podium, Mr Bell hammered home his advantage, and quoted a line from a famous philosopher[1], "Can we fix it…by fix it I mean just come up with some ideas in terms of location and layout as we won't actually be doing any of the manual work, as I am a middle-aged teacher and you are children and between us we don't have much building know-how?"

"Yes, we can!" came the reply as the children high-fived each other and jumped up and down in the sand.

So, it was, that the powers that be had unbelievably decided to let a class of ordinary children make the biggest decision about the future of the school. Unfortunately, they couldn't find any ordinary children, so Mr Bell's class was chosen instead.

The brief (not Mr Grimshaw's briefs) was simple, design a school and decide where to put it—money no object, no idea too outrageous. So, Mr Bell decided to split the children into groups to work on the project.

"Okay, so let's divide you up."

"Forty-seven, remainder three," blurted out Fred. Fred was the youngest child in the class and had a reputation for never listening to anything any teacher had ever said. However, as soon as he heard something vaguely to do with maths (when not actually in a maths lesson obviously), such as the word divide, he would instantly bang out an answer. One time, a couple of years ago, he was actually right.

1   Very catchy phrase from the philosopher Bobus the Builderus.

"Thanks Fred," Mr Bell replied encouragingly, "But actually I will split you up into four groups. To make things simple, you five boys can be group B." He gestured to a group containing Malcolm and Jack, and drew a big letter B in the sand.

"You five, with Bob as leader, can be Group B," more hand gestures and another big B drawn in the sand. "Chloe and Ellie, you will lead the best team, so to make it simple you can have a big capital B as your symbol." A third identical B was drawn in the sand.

"Finally, the remaining children are definitely brilliant, bright and bubbly group so…"

"Let me guess," shouted Jack sarcastically.

"That's right, you are team Alan, as Alan is the leader," and Mr Bell drew a massive ALAN in the sand.

"You can really see why Mr Bell is one of the best teachers in the school," said Oscar, "He has a knack of making things so simple."

So, the children shuffled off to their groups and Mr Bell watched with pride as Group B, Group B, Group B and Group Alan set to work on their plans.

The children spent the rest of the afternoon brainstorming ideas and Mr Bell went from group to group monitoring their progress. Group B wanted the school relocated somewhere in Space, perhaps in or around the Asteroid Belt (or even the Asteroid trousers). Whereas Group B's ideas concentrated on top of the tallest building in the centre of the city. However, Group B were heading for a school that could float or possibly even be based underwater. Finally, Group Alan talked about a cyber-school, with robotic teachers and virtual homework (virtually none they hoped).

As the sun was beginning to set and the tide was rapidly approaching, the groups all came together and a consensus was rapidly agreed. "Agreed," they all agreed. As much as the afternoon had been fun discussing some crazy ideas, the outcome was obvious from the start. There was only one place that the children wanted the school to be, and that was exactly in the same place that it had been previously.

So, a few short weeks later, Sandy Primary School was reopened, about one hundred metres from where Mr Bell and the children had discussed ideas, right on the edge of the beach where it had proudly stood before Soft and Fluffy tore it down.

As for the design, that was obvious too, the children wanted it to look just like it did before, three ramshackled floors, a small playground and a view to die for (not literally).

As Mr Dijon and the government big wigs cut the ribbon to officially reopen the school, the children beamed with pride at the one additional feature that they had added. Mr Bell was given the honour to hoist up Mr Grimshaw's underpants (reclaimed from the police—half-mast as a sign of respect) on Sandy Primary's brand new flagpole.

CHAPTER 02

MR X

Mr Bell picked up and turned over his special ten-minute egg timer out of his vast collection of egg-timers. "Begin," he said calmly.

"His name is Justin Styles."

It was Wednesday, which meant it was time for the Wednesday Waffle. Mr Bell had decided to hand over a ten-minute time slot to the children for discussions and observations, basically a show and tell for older children, every Wednesday morning. This meant he didn't have to teach for a precious ten minutes, so he could enjoy another cup of tea, and the Wednesday Waffle could lead to some interesting discussions. However, as usually happened, Chloe was the only child who actually brought in ideas or items to waffle about, and things tended to get a bit bonkers. Chloe stood in front of the class.

"Is he dead?" enquired Oscar.

Chloe could waffle about anything and everything. In the last few weeks, she had talked passionately about her shoe, a stone, a stone she found in her shoe, the day she lost the stone she found in her shoe and the increasing threat North Korea poses to its Asian neighbours under the leadership of Kim Jong-un.

"No, he's very much alive," and to demonstrate the point Chloe poked Justin in the ribs. Justin jumped slightly, knocking saw-dust on the floor, then sat there motionless again.

This week, Chloe had really gone to town for her waffle. She had brought in her pet guinea-pig called Justin Styles. Although she was only small, Chloe had a big personality, she blew her long blonde fringe out of her eyes and continued.

"Justin is my pet guinea-pig and as you can see he has very long hair." Justin did indeed have very long hair of various colours.

"What breed is he?" asked Alan.

"A long-haired guinea pig."

"Who'd have thought that," Mr Bell whispered sarcastically as he sipped the tea.

"Is he dead now?" asked Oscar.

All eyes on Justin, a quick poke through the cage then back to the waffle.

"Can he dance?" asked Lina.

"Does he eat cheese?" asked Malcolm.

"Has he ever been to Italy?" asked Lucy.

"Could he be used by a chimnee sweep in Lunndon?" asked Hettie.

"Can he sing?" asked Lola.

"Can he read?" asked Ellie.

"Has he ever escaped?" asked Dave.

"What's a guinea-pig?" asked Bob.

"Is he dead now?"

Yes, this was turning into every other Wednesday Waffle thought Mr Bell. It had turned bonkers again, predictably, but since he still had half a cup of tea to go, and because his egg-timer still had life in it, he decided to let Chloe carry on with her question and answer session.

"What's his favourite TV show?" asked one of the twins.

"Is he political?" asked Tim.

The questions continued thick and fast. Nobody asked why he was called Justin Styles; that was obvious, he was named after Chloe's two favourite pop-stars—Justin Perry and Taylor Styles.

"If Justin mated with a new puppy, would the baby be a Puppy New Guinea?" Jack inquired with a big smirk on his face.

Cue raucous laughter from the whole class and a chuckle from Mr Bell. This led to about five minutes of class discussion of what would happen if different animals had babies together. The top ten interesting ideas were:

A frog and a horse—a hog of frorse

A cat and a dog—a cog

A snake and a spider—a snider (who can slider) or a spake

A crab and a hippo—a crippo

A swan and a hippo—a swippo

A hen and a hippo—still a hippo (or still a hen—Mr Bell who was famed for his terrible jokes also asked where you would find hippos—at the top of your leggos)

A sheep and a kangaroo—a woolly jumper

A monkey and a donkey—a monkey or a donkey

Three point four two—that was from Fred who had heard something about halves of an animal and thought it was a maths question.

A bull and a china shop—a big mess.

The class also discussed the possibility of crossing a duck and a platypus and came up with the idea of duck-billed platypus, but everyone thought that was just too silly.

"My mum said that a lion can actually have a baby with a tiger, and you get a real animal," Kyle pipped up.

"Liger," Mr Bell replied.

"No, it's definitely true."

"Okay, okay, enough, enough," Mr Bell stood up accidentally knocking his finished egg-timer on the floor. "I think we should all thank Chloe for this enlightening Waffle session, and I have certainly learnt a lot. Nothing about guinea-pig care obviously, but I do now know a sure-fire test to see if one is alive." And he poked Justin through the bars of the cage whilst slurping the last of his tea.

The children all groaned, as they all loved the Wednesday Waffle as much as Mr Bell did, ten minutes without being taught anything was as precious to them as it was to Mr Bell not having to teach them anything.

"We need to move on because it will be assembly soon, but more importantly because, I am sorry to have to say this Justin, but frankly, you stink." All eyes on Justin, a quick poke to test his level of dead-ness by Chloe, and nods of agreement from the whole class. "Unless, we are being unfair to Justin and Malcolm has been blowing off again," continued Mr Bell.

Malcolm was a short boy, with a round face and rounder belly and he had a fearsome reputation for having the trumpiest trousers in Sandy Primary. He sat at the back of the class and the whole class slowly turned to look at him. However, he looked genuinely hurt by the accusation and stared at Mr Bell with his big, brown cow eyes and shook his head disbelievingly.

"Sorry Malcolm, just checking, definitely Justin then," Mr Bell replied suspiciously.

Malcolm nodded his head in approval to the apology, then turned around to Jack and mouthed, "I've been chuffing like a train all morning!"

Jack mouthed back whilst putting his thumbs in the air, "So have I!"

Mr Bell smiled to himself, he loved Wednesdays, not only for the bonus cuppa during the Waffle but next up was assembly, and another half an hour or so of tea drinking whilst Mr X took charge.

"Therefore," continued Mr Bell. "I think Justin could do with some fresh air, it's a lovely breezy day today, and our classroom can be aired during assembly."

So, Chloe and her best friend Lina who was twice her size, awkwardly carried the cage towards the back door of the classroom.

"How will we know if he is dead if he is outside the classroom?" asked Oscar.

"I am positive Justin will be fine, and we can use Chloe's patented poking method every hour or so to make sure," said Mr Bell as he tidied away his slightly dented egg-timer.

"Yes, but what if he escapes," asked one of the twins.

"Look, what are the chances of Chloe and Lina actually being daft enough to leave the cage door open as soon as he is out of sight, and Justin being smart enough to actually escape?" chuckled Mr Bell.

"No chance, impossible, slim at best, twenty-seven (Fred again), do me a favour, against all odds," were some of the replies from the giggling class.

However, just outside the back door of the classroom, Chloe and Lina left the cage door open and Justin Styles promptly escaped.

What were the odds of that happening? In Sandy Primary, pretty, pretty high.

Meanwhile, up in his office on the top floor of Sandy Primary, the Principal, Mr X, was preparing for the weekly assembly. The usual rules and reminders to talk about, and unfortunately, as often happened, kid's good old friends, head-lice, had made a comeback to the infant classes.

He was going through his usual nit-prevention speech in his head and flicking through his phone to see if he still had the number of the government nurse, Nitty Nora the Head Explorer as she was affectionately known, in case she needed to pay a visit.

He chuckled to himself, the same issues every year kept coming up; he loved his job, the school, and the children and really took a great deal of pride in seeing how the kids grew and matured. However, recently, this pride was beginning to be tinged with slight sadness as Mr X was growing older too each day and much wider around the tummy.

A little bit of background on Sandy Primary's principal. His full name was Gheorghe Andrei Vladimir Xenodocheionology[2] (the third o is silent obviously). His father (Vladimir Vladislav Vsevolod Wayne Xenodocheionology) had been a failed collector of antiquities in Moldova. The family joke was that he spent way too much time collecting letters and not enough on artefacts. Apart from an extremely long name, he had also inherited his father's love of learning and history and it was a natural step for him to become a teacher.

---

2   This is not just a brilliantly entertaining story, it's a chance to learn too—please look up this word, there will be a test next Friday.

No one ever attempted to pronounce his name (even his mother, whose maiden name was Jane Smith). So, for all his life, his friends called him George and when he became a teacher, the nickname Mr X soon stuck.

He secretly loved his nickname, as it gave him a mysterious dimension, which could always be used in his favour. *You'll be off to see Mr X if you don't behave.* For children who didn't know him well, it sounded like they were off to see a Bond Villain, and usually it did the trick to get them behaving again.

He often heard the children discussing what the X actually stood for. X marks the spot, X-box, X-ray, X-cellent, X-periment (on naughty children), X-pert, X-pell (always a good one) X-ecution (great to put fear in the infants) and X-it (as he often stood by the door). Also, some kids thought he was called Mr Cross, he even heard one young boy saying his surname was Crosses and his first names were definitely *Noughts And*. In reality, Mr X was kind and reliable and was a big softy once you got to know him. He had worked at Sandy Primary for donkey's years.

To try to reduce his ever-increasing waistline, his wife had started putting healthy snacks into his jacket pocket every day, as Mr X had a weakness for vending machines and less healthy options. It was a lovely idea, and every time he worried about anything or felt a bit peckish, his right hand would automatically be attracted to his pocket where he would find some nuts, dried fruit or other organic treats.

"Yum, raisins," he muttered to himself as his hand came out of his pocket and he popped a handful into his mouth. "Thanks love, erm…not you, Ms. Andrews." He said the last bit a tad too loud, just as the school secretary had tottered into his office, in her extremely large high heels and plonked some papers on the desk. She looked at him strangely and quickly tottered out again.

Mr X could handle his expanding waistline (literally) and he realised he never even saw Ms. Andrews entering his office, so maybe it was time to get his eyes checked too. These were practical issues that he could hopefully resolve but he had a much more worrying issue of which he felt very uncomfortable. He had a dark secret. Dark secret is not technically true, it was more a brown, silver, black and just a touch of ginger secret. You see, Mr X wore a wig. In his youth, he had had thick, long, wavy, luscious locks of many wonderful hues. But sadly, it had thinned and thinned like a dying bush in a desert, until about five years ago, after the summer break, he made a hair-raising (well, hair-changing) decision. He had walked back into school wearing his super-toupee (as a big ABBA fan, he called it his super-touper). It was very striking. All the staff knew, but no one said anything or really cared, as Mr X was such a nice guy. Occasionally, jokes about *X-hair, the job's gone to his head, brave decision—very bald* or the *bald head of the school;* could be heard (or even haired) in the staffroom. However, after a few weeks everything seemed normal and Mr X began to relax.

He ran his fingers through his multi-coloured falsie and glanced out of the window. He saw Mr Grimshaw's undies flapping quite violently and gulped as he realised his nemesis had returned to haunt him...wind!

The wind had obviously destroyed the school not long ago, and over the last hour or so it had picked up quite considerably. He wasn't concerned about the school blowing over, however, he was always paranoid about a wig-in-the-wind situation and the potential embarrassment that could cause to him. Luckily, on the day of the hurricane, he had been on Mr Dijon's yacht discussing school business, and miles away from danger. As he glanced up again at the flagpole, he was incredibly relieved that he wasn't there that fateful day, as his wig could be blowing up there too, next to the pants.

Still, he had a problem now, assembly was held on the middle floor in the Assembly Room. Technically, the Assembly Room was just a spare classroom, minus the desks and chairs. Ms. Andrews had posted a label on the door in big letters that said ASSEMBLY ROOM. Underneath, someone (possibly Jack) had written *not just an empty classroom.* Mr X would have to get down there within the next five minutes without any hair-piece mishaps, so he would have to brave the elements.

What were the chances that as soon as he stepped out of his office, a freak breeze would whip off his super-touper and leave him looking like a baldy lemon? He stood up and chuckled, *no chance,* impossible, slim at best, (twenty-seven would be an answer that Fred would probably have given), do me a favour, against all odds. So, he opened his office door and confidently stepped out, just as a freak breeze whizzed in, whipped off his super-touper (like a super-touper, my bald head gonna blind you) and left him looking like a baldy lemon.

What were the odds of that happening? In Sandy Primary, pretty high.

Panic! Absolute panic, this is not a picnic, this is panic!

Mr X helplessly watched as his wig floated away on the breeze, it was then blown over the roof and out of sight. Incredibly, it hovered down and landed bang in the middle of Justin Style's cage. More incredibly, at exactly the same time Justin popped his head around the corner of the school and after a good session of eating greenery around the back of the building, he decided this would be a perfect time for a snooze in the sun.

In Mr X's absolute panic-ridden state and with his less than perfect eyes, Justin looked like his toupee had just come back to him, like a hairy boomerang. Quick as a flash, he grabbed a glue-stick from his desk and rushed down the stairs. He could hear the scraping of chairs from all the classrooms around him, a sure sign that at any second all the children would be on the move to the assembly room, and he would be caught with his wig down.

With seconds to spare, he sprinted across the playground, scooped up Justin in his left hand and instantaneously smeared his under-belly with glue with his right hand and rapidly plonked him on his baldy bonce.

Justin threatened to wake up, but was quite happy laying across Mr X's head. Justin's head lay over Mr X's left ear, and his bottom hovered above Mr X's right ear.

Mr X was so relieved to find his wig, he didn't notice he had a rodent on his head, he was just aware it didn't feel quite right, so he hastily decided to rush through assembly and make a sharp exit afterwards to adjust himself. He took a deep breath and headed upstairs.

Meanwhile, fresh cup of tea in hand, Mr Bell was quietening the assembled assembly down, the children were more or less settled so he walked over to door to check if Mr X was on his way.

Mr Bell nearly dropped his tea when Mr X's face appeared at the door, his face was not unusual but the guinea-pig glued to his head certainly was. Mr Bell opened the door, his bottom-lip almost touching the floor in shock.

"Arr, Mr Bell, lots on today, could you do the usual rules and things? I just want a very, very quick chat with the children about hair." Mr X said very routinely.

Mr Bell just stared, he tried to speak but couldn't, it was only when some of his tea spilt on his foot that he was able to respond with a grunt and slight nod of his head.

"Jolly good," Mr X replied and walked over to face the children.

Silence, absolute silence.

The children gawped at Mr X in complete shock, they gaped at Mr Bell who goggled back at them.

"Nice and quiet, marvellous. Now a quick word. Hair. If you have anything in your hair that makes you itch or scratch, please tell your parents, we don't want any uninvited guests entering the school do we?" chuckled Mr X.

Silence, absolute silence.

"Any questions?"

Mr Bell had slightly come out of his state of shock and stared at the children, he shook his head, pleading with them not to speak. There was no need, the children were still ogling Mr X in a complete trance.

All through this bizarre spectacle, Justin kept falling in and out of consciousness, every time he briefly woke, he expelled a small pellet of poop that popped out of his bum, dropped past Mr X's ear and landed in the principal's right-hand pocket of his jacket. This seemed to hypnotise his audience even more, they watched awe-struck at the novelty-act that stood in front of them.

"Great, well, I will be off then, Mr Bell will continue with the assembly. Remember, keep an eye on your hair!" With that Mr X quickly walked to the door. The children were not keeping an eye on their hair, then had both eyes on his.

Mr X trotted out of the assembly room and as soon as he was out of sight, he gave an enormous sigh of relief and leaned against the wall. I may have just got away with that he thought to himself. Instinctively, his right hand reached into his jacket pocket. With all the stress, an extra big handful of raisins was in order.

It wasn't until the next day when Chloe was invited in before school started, the exchange of the slightly gluey Justin, for a slightly saw-dusty toupee, that the whole story could be pieced together. Mr X was obviously embarrassed by the whole episode and left school early that day. Not because of the inevitable gossip, but because for some strange reason, he had developed a terrible stomach-ache overnight.

CHAPTER 03

THE REAL GAMES ROOM LOSER

Tim was obsessed. Completely obsessed. Obsessed completely with entering the Games Room.

The original Sandy Primary had a small classroom on the ground floor in which the children could play games at lunch and break time. It was a grotty little place to be honest. It contained some small pool tables and a battered-up table football game. It also had loads of games and jigsaw puzzles which were so old and had been so badly treated by the children, that not one of them contained all of the pieces.

When the children designed the new school, they did design a new and improved games room. Unfortunately, most of the budget had been used up when it came to kitting it out. So, Mr Dijon, the school owner had an extremely tricky decision, either a new speedboat that would fit nicely on the back of his yacht, or a state of the art games room for the children. After much soul-searching, he plumped for the speedboat.

Therefore, the children were presented with a new, small classroom on the ground floor but all the old games and puzzles from before the rebuild. Even though the room itself was new, it still felt small and grotty.

This didn't put the children off the games room, it was an extremely popular place to be. Not only the dog-eared games that were still fun to play but it had another great draw. In the winter, it had a lovely warm heater that could be switched on, and in the summer months, it had a fully functional air-conditioner. The children were supposed to be outside at lunch and break time, so if the weather wasn't too good, it made a lovely haven to hang out with friends.

However, there was a catch. It wasn't free to enter.

As it had become so popular, Mr X had concocted a devious, devilish plan. In an attempt to stop the children from killing each other, he had decreed that good behaviour would be rewarded with a precious games room voucher (and entry for one day into the room). Whereas bad behaviour (including murder) would lead to loss of vouchers and therefore, no entry. The vouchers were small and green, and were the nearest thing to money that the children had.

Tim was obsessed. Completely obsessed. Obsessed completely with entering the Games Room.

Of course, the games were a pull, who doesn't like playing Risk with no dice or Twister on a sheet so faded you can't see any colours? And what's not to like about heat when it's cold or cold when it's hot? But these were not the reasons Tim yearned to enter it. The real reason was power.

The feeling of power that entered his body when he set foot in the room was intoxicating to him. *Non-games room losers* he would snigger to himself whilst prancing up and down past the window that overlooked the playground. This was often accompanied by the internationally recognised *loser* sign, by placing his left thumb and forefinger on his forehead.

Out there in the heat, Games Room Loser!

Or

Out there in the cold, Games Room Loser!

These were Tim's favourite sayings, he would sneer at the unfortunate children who didn't have a voucher to enter the room as he peacocked past the windows. In fact, Tim very rarely played any of the games or appreciated the comfortable temperatures, he was far too busy pointing out to anyone who would listen that he was inside the room, whilst others were not.

Yes, Tim was obsessed. Completely obsessed. Obsessed completely with entering the Games Room.

It was a Monday. Tim didn't have any vouchers left. So, he was on a mission to get some.

"Mr Bell, can I have a games room voucher please?"

"No, you can't."

"Can I buy one off you," Tim gestured towards his pocket.

"No, you can't."

"Can I swap one for one of my sandwiches?"

"No, you can't...erm...what flavour?"

"Cheese."

"No, you can't."

"Please!"

"Look Tim, I am not exaggerating here, but I have told you a million times that you have to earn the vouchers, they are not for sale and besides, I don't like cheese." Mr Bell was standing at the entrance to his classroom and it was five to nine so school was about to start.

Tim looked at Mr Bell with his best puppy dog eyes, "Pretty please?" he begged.

"Don't do the eyes Tim!" Mr Bell covered his eyes so he wasn't drawn into Tim's emotional blackmail. "I am sure you can earn some today, you are a clever lad. Now what about your homework, have you finished it yet?"

Mr Bell was, of course, right. Tim was very bright, he had a great general knowledge and usually did well in class. Homework was always collected on Friday but a voucher could be earned by handing it in early.

"Oh, yes, yes, I forgot," squealed Tim and he rushed to his bag to find it.

"Put it in the homework tray and I will check it in a moment."

Tim plonked it in the green tray that was situated right by the door of the classroom and did a little jump of delight whilst mouthing, "Yes, get in!"

With that, Chloe, who was the bell monitor, rang the bell. As this was Sandy Primary School though, they didn't actually have a bell.

The phrase, *has the bell gone?* could well have originated at Sandy Primary as the bell had been nicked a long time ago. So, the answer was yes, the bell has well gone!

It was the role of the bell monitor to go around the playground shouting *Ding-Dong*.

"Ding-dong, ding-dong!" Chloe screamed at the top of her voice, although she was only small, she had a booming voice.

"Okay, okay, settle in, settle down," said Mr Bell[3] as the children barged into the classroom and began to sit down. "Hands up if you are not here today," he chuckled as he scanned the room and marked off the register. This was another of his daily awful jokes and the children all groaned. One of the identical twins was off but no one was sure which one, so Mr Bell guessed. It could have been Kath who was a small girl with black hair, or Kim who was a tall boy with blonde hair but even the twin who was there didn't really know.

"First things first, if anyone has handed their homework in early, they will receive a coveted games room voucher." He walked over to the green homework tray and picked up a small stack of papers. "Good job, Lucy, Ellie, Lola. Erm...Dave this is actually your mum's shopping list and well-done Bob for handing in your worksheet, but you were supposed to answer the questions."

"Really?" said Bob, "I don't remember you saying we had to actually answer them!"

Dave chuckled to himself as he imagined his mum in the supermarket with his angles worksheet.

"There is one more here..."

"Mine, mine, Mr Bell," Tim called out whilst jumping up and down in his seat with his hand raised.

"Ah! Yes, one more here, sadly without a name, I recognise your writing Tim but you know the rules, no name means loss of a

---

3   By the way Mr Bell was not related to The School Bell although it was often said that a bit like Quasimodo, his face rang a bell. At school his nickname had been Dumb Bell. Kids can be cruel sometimes, although to be fair it was the teachers that used it more often.

voucher, so I will have to take it back." With that Mr Bell dangled a voucher in front of Tim and then dramatically pulled it back as Tim tried to grab it.

Tim's elation had rapidly turned to despair.

"Right gang, first up today is maths," Mr Bell announced after he had put down the homework stack and picked up his tea (his fifth of the day).

"I love maths, yes, I love learning numbers and facts," Lola suddenly sang in a very theatrical way. Lola was the second smallest but most musical member of the class, she loved singing and she loved maths.

The class all giggled.

"I love that you love maths Lola and I love your enthusiasm, here have a games room voucher," Mr Bell replied whilst walking over to Lola's desk and handing her a voucher.

"I love maths too…erm…I like learning forty-seven multiplied by two," Tim blurted out in a sorry attempt to copy Lola's singing road to voucher success. It sounded a bit like a mad man squeezing a cat in the belief that they were bag-pipes. Singing certainly wasn't Tim's strong point.

The class all looked at Tim in horror and disbelief. Even Ellie looked up from her reading book, briefly.

"Stone the crows," Hattie muttered sadly to herself.

"Tim what have I told you about shouting out and telling lies? That's minus two vouchers I'm afraid."

"I didn't shout, I sang."

"Ah that's what it was, okay, good point, only minus one voucher then."

"And I do kind of like maths," Tim said aloud.

"Fair enough, back to zero then, although technically you did just shout out then, so unfortunately, you are back to negative one voucher again," Mr Bell said matter-of-factly.

All lesson Tim gained and lost vouchers, he got more and more frustrated as others seemed to gain vouchers with ease whilst he didn't. After a roller-coaster ride, at break time he was completely exhausted and had a massive total of zero vouchers earned.

As he looked enviously at the packed-out games room, he was more determined than ever to get a precious voucher. Ellie was just about to enter the Games Room, book in hand, and Tim saw his chance.

"Hey Ellie, give us one of your vouchers, I haven't got any and I know you have got loads."

Ellie stopped and stared at Tim. "Here's what you need to do, cry yourself a river, build yourself a bridge and get over it!" With that she continued into the Games Room and dramatically slammed the door in Tim's face.

"That's just charming," Tim looked around the playground, his only other friends who weren't inside the Games Room were Kyle and Alan.

"Kyle, can you lend me a Games Room voucher?"

"My mum says that the Games Room voucher system is deeply flawed, and kids should learn to do things for their own pride, not a silly reward," replied Kyle.

"Your mum is very wise, so you might as well give me some of yours then."

"My mum says, never lend or borrow things, and besides I don't have any."

Tim shook his head in annoyance and homed in on Alan.

"I haven't got any," Alan took a pre-emptive strike as Tim wandered over.

"Okay, okay, so what's the next lesson, Al?"

"I think Mr Bell said we would be doing history," Alan replied as he took a huge bite out of his tuna sandwich.

Great. Tim didn't really love maths but he genuinely loved history. He was great at remembering names and facts and he particularly loved the old Tudor Kings and Queens that they were currently studying. He felt the executions were a fair system of keeping order and he was sure he would have reached the dizzy heights of Keeper of the Stool—the King's official bum wiper and close confidant. A bum job but you got close to the king, exceedingly close, could have been a cracking job in fact.

He knew if he stayed calm and showed Mr Bell how much knowledge he had, it was bound to impress him and he would have a load of vouchers come lunch time.

"Is Henry VIII dead or is he still alive?" Oscar asked when they were all back in class.

"Well, if he is still alive, he would be about six hundred years old," Mr Bell replied chortling.

"So, he is dead then, really dead like Mr Grimshaw," Oscar smiled mischievously.

"Yes, we can well and truly say he is pushing up the daisies, Henry that is, not Mr Grimshaw!"

"Is it true Henry VI, had eight wives?" inquired Lina.

"No, everyone knows Henry VIII had ten wives," interrupted Lucy.

"That's right," Jack piped up. "And there's a rhyme to remember what happened to them...it's divorced, beheaded, got lost, divorced, beheaded and chopped, divorced again for sure, her head was found on the floor, two more didn't survive, last one called Kylie's, still alive!"

Hoots of laughter from the class but Tim just sat there in disbelief at the stream of nonsense being spoken in front of him. However, he bit his lip and was focused on choosing the right moment to get into Mr Bell's good books and get his richly deserved voucher.

"Nice try Jack, here have a voucher, but you are right some of Henry's six wives did end up in half," Mr Bell chuckled.

"Zero point seven-five," burst out Fred having again heard something vaguely mathematical.

"Good effort Fred."

Fred went back to his happy place. His happy place of paying absolutely no attention at all.

"I saw this program on TV that said the Tudors died out because of a meteor strike...or was that the dinosaurs?" Dave inquired.

"That was definitely the dinosaurs, my mum told me, they died out about a hundred years or so before the Tudors," Kyle declared. "Just after Buzz Lightyear landed on the moon and Columbus invented the telephone."

"What's a T-rex's favourite song?" Lola suddenly shouted out. "If you're happy and you know it clap your hands!"

The whole class joined in whilst pretending to have tiny T-Rex arms, even Mr Bell had a go.

"Stop this you morons!" Tim suddenly screamed. He could take it no longer and had exploded with rage. "The Tudors ruled from 1485 to 1603, their reign finished as Elizabeth never had children. Henry VIII had six wives, two of whom were executed. The dinosaurs died out about sixty-five and a half million years ago, possibly by a meteor strike." He was standing up now and his face had turned a funny purple colour. "Neil Armstrong and Buzz Aldrin landed on the moon in 1969, Columbus was an explorer who sailed to The Americas in 1492 and the telephone was invented by flipping Alexander Graham Bell, and stop being T-Rexes!"

Silence. Complete Silence. Silence completely.

A stunned class of dinosaurs stared at Tim, who suddenly wished he was extinct.

As Mr Bell's entire class luxuriated in the Games Room at lunchtime, fair reward for their enthusiasm (if not for their factual knowledge) during their history discussion. Tim was elsewhere.

He had air-con and a heater and plenty of windows to look out of but not a lot else. For Tim spent that lunchtime and many, many more after that in detention in Mr X's office. History would judge that he was the real Games Room loser!

CHAPTER 04

A Bunch of Complete and Utter Idioms

"Is this meant to be funny?"

Clang.

"Is it?"

"No, it's meant to be my homework?"

"Would you like to read out your homework to the class?"

"Why have you forgotten your glasses?"

It was a Friday morning and Mr Bell was planning to start his Literacy lesson about everyday expressions. However, he had been well and truly side-lined…something had come up…he had lost his thread. [4]

"Don't push your luck Jack, you are in enough trouble already."

Thud.

Mr Bell's left temple began to throb. This happened when the usually calm Mr Bell got stressed. It was certainly visible today because of Jack's behaviour. Also, he was really straining his eyes because as Jack had helpfully pointed out, he *had* forgotten his glasses.

The reason Mr Bell had gone off on a tangent was because before Literacy every Friday, he usually had a quick check over of the class homework. This was usually a brief session to ensure

---

4   This amazing book, is once again earning its keep by being tip-top and educational. This chapter is jam packed, full to brimming if you will, with everyday expressions or idioms. So be on your guard and if this book is not borrowed from a library please feel free to highlight them as you journey through this chapter. Best of British to you!

names were written on and games room vouchers handed out (see previous chapter if you have forgotten). However, today was different. Mr Bell had had a tip-off from, well, all the other teachers in the school, that Jack's homework was in need of a much more thorough examination.

"OK, smart Alec, I will remind you of your homework remit, some ideas I gave you and some of your friends' ideas, then maybe you would be so kind to share yours with the class?" Mr Bell wiped his brow and leaned over his desk to pick up the stack of homework that the other children had handed in.

"It would be my pleasure," replied Jack who was calmly standing opposite Mr Bell, his black floppy hair covering the top of his eyes.

"So," Mr Bell continued, placing his left hand over his temple, "I am sure you recall last week that we were doing tally charts and bar charts."

"I do, as if it were only last week!"

"It was Jack, and I'm also sure that you will remember that I asked you to create your own tally charts and bar charts."

"I was all over it."

Clang.

"My ideas included a survey of favourite TV shows, crisp flavours, football players and so on and so forth."

Jack mused for a second and replied, "Having given it a great deal of thought, I would have to plump for Belgium's Got Talent, Haggis and Hedgehog flavour, and come on the mighty Wayne Looney!"

Mr Bell was trying desperately to keep his legendary patience. "Therefore, let us see what other ideas the class managed to come up with," Mr Bell looked down at the pile of paper in his hand, "Tim has created a wonderful graph of who won games room vouchers this week." Mr Bell held up Tim' work. "Well done Tim, two vouchers for you, although looking in more detail, you didn't use a ruler, so that will cost you two." (Again, please see Chapter 3 for full details of how Tim will likely take the news).

"Ellie has produced a graph of how many books she read, it's an enormous straight line with the word LOTS written on it, thanks Ellie," Mr Bell muttered sarcastically. As usual, Ellie wasn't really paying attention, she had her head in a book.

Other class member's work included how many twins I have, answer one. This was either by Kath, who was a small girl with black hair or her tall, blond haired twin-brother Kim, but as they were identical, no one was sure which one. Hettie had produced a relevant piece of work with a graph entitled 'How Many Children where maimed or killed in Workhouse related accidents in 1873 in London'. 'How many dead animals I have seen this week' was Oscar's offering and Chloe had taken things literally and listed all the bars, her dad had visited during the week. Fred came up with an answer of nine point one four six two.

"Mmmm, to be honest Mr Bell," Jack stated whilst rubbing his chin, "I have to say my work is much better, it combines both maths with science and provides a fascinating insight into human behaviour."

Mr Bell was on the ragged edge, the examples he had chosen, hadn't really helped his cause and Jack's graphs were extremely neat, and extremely clever, but Mr Bell was feeling the heat from the rest of the staff members and he couldn't let him off the hook.

Clunk.

"Jack, please read your title to the class."

"For sure, the title is, my tally Chart and Bar Graph of what happened when I hit other people in the playground."

There were a few giggles and gasps from the class. "I don't think I quite understand Jack," said an exasperated Mr Bell.

"Oh, it's quite simple really, I went around...in my own time, I may add, hitting others...pretty hard, and recording the results in a tally chart, which I then interpreted in a bar graph."

More gasps and giggles.

"What...how?"

"With my fists."

"No Jack, what an earth were you thinking and how can any of this be a good idea?" Mr Bell wobbled slightly and had to hold on to his desk for support, as if his morning was going badly enough, he hadn't had time for his third cup of tea and was getting withdrawal symptoms.

Jack faced the class, "It was a fascinating insight into the human psyche, as you can see from my findings, thirty-seven percent of people hit me back, forty-two percent cried, seventeen percent called their teacher, two percent were hospitalised, one percent hit me with her book (no prizes for guessing who), one percent threatened me with blackmail if I didn't give him all my games room vouchers (all eyes on Tim) and one percent took me to his office."

"What!"

"Yeah, looking back, maybe I shouldn't have hit Mr X but I always go that extra mile for my research."

The class fell silent, a sense of shock descended.

"That makes a hundred and one percent."

Everyone turned and looked at Fred, if anything could make a shocked class even more shocked, it was the shocking realisation that Fred was spot on with his calculations.

The shockingly, shocked, silence was broken by another huge Clang!

Dave was tall and gangly and he sat at the very front of the class, he was a popular boy, with many great friends. He was also the untidiest human that had ever lived. His desk was a no-go area, the class had christened it Dave's Desk of Doom. Items that had recently been spotted there included an old sock, an empty yogurt pot, banana peel, some Ancient Egyptian artefacts and legend suggested that a squirrel called it home.

All through the lesson, items had been falling out of his desk and bouncing on the floor, a ruler, a set of false teeth, a fishing rod and finally a set of dumb bells (not a collection of Mr Bells but real dumb bells used for weight-lifting).

Mr Bell, having enough on his plate with Jack, had been trying his best to ignore these interruptions. But enough was enough.

Mr Bell surveyed his class, Jack and his antics, Dave and his junk yard, Ellie head in a book as usual, he'd reached breaking point. He could contain his rage no longer.

"You lot are a bunch of idiots!" he screamed, his hand outstretched and his fingers seemed to be squeezing an invisible child's neck. Steam appeared to be coming from his ears.

Silence...clunk (remote control this time)...almost absolute silence.

Mr Bell was on the ropes but recovered some composure, "As I said, you lot are a bunch of *Idioms*, and unless any of you are recording this, you can't prove I said anything else."

He looked around the room pointing aggressively at his band of bonkers pupils. "And I have some predictions for you. Ellie the book-worm, having your head in a book, believe me, one day will lead you to have a hideous accident. Dave, your dangerous, disgusting desk of doom is going to land you in hot water my friend, sooner than you think. And Jack, as for you, you are off the scale in terms of craziness, you'd better pull your socks up my lad or the men in white coats are going to come in here one day and carry you out."

Clang (a small model of the Eiffel Tower).

"Arggggggggggg! I need a break, I need a cup of tea, I am going to get the kettle," with that Mr Bell stormed out of his own classroom. Well he nearly did, as the red mist had descended.

And as he wasn't really thinking or seeing straight, he stormed right into the storeroom. The storeroom door was right next to the exit door. After what seemed like a lifetime, Mr Bell quietly opened the storeroom door, composed himself, and then stormed out of his own classroom. The idiom, when one door closes another one opens, would be appropriate.

"What's wrong with Mr Bell?" said Lola.

"Bit over the top, if you ask me," Jack declared.

Meanwhile, up on the top floor, Mr X was an incredibly happy man. Today was injection day!

Having loads of young children in a state of panic before being subjected to a painful stab in the arm, would obviously fill any head-teacher with joy. But that wasn't the reason he was so joyful. Being able to crack terrible jokes about rusty needles, would also make any responsible adult all contented. But that wasn't the reason either. No, the reason was Mr X was going to be reunited with the person who he thought had the best name in the world.

Mr X could see him on the CCTV entering the school, and just then Miss Andrews, the school secretary confirmed the good news.

"Dr Hoo is here Mr X to do the annual vaccinations. Shall I show him in?"

This is what Mr X had waited for and he nodded his head up and down like an excited puppy.

Dr Hoo was the local doctor and always came to Sandy Primary to do the injections. He walked up to the top floor and then knocked on Mr X's door.

"Say it."

"Do we have to go through this every time I come here?"

"Please!"

"But I just knocked, it doesn't make any sense for me to say it, and it's a glass door, so you can see me."

"Say it!"

"Alright, alright if it means we can get on with things...knock, knock."

"Who's there?" Mr X put his hands over his mouth in excitement.

"Dr Hoo," replied Dr Hoo.

"No, do it properly!"

"Oh, come on...Knock, knock."

"Who's there?"

"Doctor," said Dr Hoo with a minimum amount of enthusiasm.

"Dr Who?" squealed Mr X.

"Yes, Dr Hoo, can I come in now?"

Mr X was doubled over in hysterics, and he gestured to Dr Hoo to come in.

"That never gets old," mumbled Dr Hoo mockingly as he entered the office.

Mr X was just regaining his composure and was breathing heavily, he looked quizzically at the doctor, "Where is your doctor's coat?"

"It's in my bag, it tends to scare the children when I enter the school and I will put it on now." Dr Hoo reached into his bag and grabbed his white lab-coat. "So…things are looking good here, I see, last time I was here, was the day of the storm, checking for injuries."

"Yes, we had a lucky escape there, well except for Mr Grimshaw obviously."

"Yes, strange what happened to him, in fact strange day all around with the storm and the bank robbery in town just afterwards."

"Indeed, indeed," Mr X looked curiously at the doctor, "Are you by yourself today? Dr Payne not with you?"

"No, Dr Payne is on holiday, my new assistant is on his way up now."

With that, Miss Andrews promptly opened the door, "Mr X, Dr Watt is here."

"What?" Mr X nearly collapsed.

"Dr Watt is here with Dr Hoo," she replied.

"What!" Mr X nearly wet himself, this was too good to be true.

"Oh yes, and he is here with Nurse Howe."

Mr X fainted.

Back on the ground floor, Mr Bell had boiled the kettle in the staffroom and was heading back to his classroom. He paused and decided to take a final mental health break on the beach. He opened the gate and stepped directly onto the sand. He took a huge gulp of fresh air, and looked up at the sky. As he wasn't wearing his glasses, which were the type that doubled as sunglasses, this dazzled him a bit and he needed to shield his eyes with his free hand as he turned and walked towards his door.

In his absence, Jack thought it would be a good idea to get back into Mr Bell's good books and would meet him at the door.

"Look, Mr Bell, I am literally pulling my socks up," Jack jumped out from behind the door and announced just as Mr Bell opened it.

"What?" Mr Bell said, swerving past Jack and heading towards his desk, kettle in hand, still half blinded from the sun. As he spun past Jack, Ellie was walking past Dave's desk and as usual she had her head in book. She accidentally knocked Dave's desk and another item fell from it. This time a tennis ball plopped out. It bounced right in front of Mr Bell who didn't see it rolling towards him. Time seemed to stand still when he slipped on it, he went flying up in the air as did his kettle.

The kettle smashed down and the hapless teacher landed in the pool of boiling water, knocking himself out in the process.

And so, it was, Mr Bell's predictions came true...sort of. Ellie having her head in the book had led to a hideous accident (just not for her).

Dave's desk of doom, didn't land him in hot water, but it did for Mr Bell, quite literally. Jack wasn't carried out of the school by the men in white coats but Mr Bell was (along with Mr X who hadn't recovered from the excitement of earlier) by the two doctors.

Mr Bell, what a complete and utter idiom!

CHAPTER 05

FUND RAISING

"My mum said this is dangerous, in fact, she said it's probably illegal."

"Oh, be quiet Kyle, just get in," replied Lola.

"What if it breaks?"

"Kyle, this is the highlight of the entire day," said Dave, "Just relax."

"Here he comes!"

"Good morning little people, jump on and off we go!"

"Morning Michael, let's go!" screamed all of the kids (except Kyle) and they threw their bags on then jumped on the Sandy Primary School, School Bus. Kyle and bag were bundled on board and Michael sped off.

Now, since this was Sandy Primary School, school bus is a very loose term. It had been a good few months since the school had reopened and a lot of money had been spent to make sure everything was back to normal.

However, the budget had been used up, the last few pennies had gone on second hand jigsaws for the games room. Mr Dijon, the school owner, had texted from his private jet that he was very sorry but there was no money left.

On the day of the hurricane, all attention was obviously on the damage to the school and the disappearance of Mr Grimshaw. Strangely, the Sandy Primary School bus had been found burned out, a few miles from the City Bank. In all the chaos, no one really wondered how it got there. But it was clear that a new bus would be needed.

The original bus was the typical yellow school bus type and it was driven by Michael. Michael was the friendliest man who has ever lived. He was tall and lanky with long, black curly hair and always wore sunglasses, whatever the weather. No one was quite sure of his age, the kids had narrowed it down to somewhere between eighteen and seventy-five. He loved to play music on the school bus and the kids loved him. High-fives and high jinks were the order of the day.

When the school was reopened, Michael was re-employed (there would have been a riot if he hadn't) but the mode of transport became a huge issue.

There was an emergency meeting a few hours before the school reopened to try to find a solution. As the school is so remote, most of the children needed a school bus to get there. No vehicles could be found but luckily Kath and Kim's (the twins) father was a pilot and he said that he could get his hands on an old-style baggage truck from the airport[5]. Mr X was very reluctant but had no choice but to accept the offer.

So, on the first day when the school reopened, Michael rolled up to the first bus-stop driving a rusty old baggage truck. It had a small cab at the front where Michael and his stereo sat, and behind it were six even rustier metal cages, that would usually house rucksacks and suitcases linked together with flimsy cables.

It took about three seconds before the kids knew that this would be the most ridiculous and the most electrifying thing that they would ever do, so they all jumped in the cages and held on for dear life. Without seat belts or much structure to the vehicle, some thought it was a potential death-trap. The good news though is that it had plenty of room for the children's bags.

It was an instant hit with the kids, just before arriving at the beach and school, there was a very steep hill that the bus had to get down. Every day the cages snaked at high speed down the hill and when the children got to school they were dizzy with delight and ready to learn. Mr X had noticed that the children's behaviour had improved since the baggage bus had been in operation, so he was happy to keep it. As long as there wasn't a terrible accident on

5   In a completely unrelated incident, all flights were delayed at the local airport as the baggage truck had gone missing and the baggage handlers had to load everything by hand.

the way to school that is. What were the chances of that happening to the Sandy Primary Baggage Bus?

"Okay gang, we are at the top of the hill," screamed Michael and he turned off the music.

This was the usual routine at it was the cue for Lola to take charge. Lola and her friends always grabbed the first baggage cage and when they reached the summit she would stand up and sing. She would be steadied by Hettie holding her left leg and Ellie holding her right one. This was the only time Ellie didn't have her head in a book as it was far too bumpy for her to focus on the words. Lola would face the children in the other cages and make up some bonkers songs to famous tunes. She would start and everyone else would join in. Today was an old favourite, *The Wheels on the Bus.*

"The wheels on the baggage bus go round and round, round and round, round and round, look at the danger we are inches from the ground, inches from the ground, inches from the ground..."

"...If we crash then we're all gonna die, all gonna die, all gonna die..."

"Only joking Kyle, please don't cry, please don't cry, please don't cry..."

"...It's like we are on a helter skelter, helter skelter, helter skelter, driving around in an Anderson Shelter, Anderson Shelter, Anderson Shelter..."

Now Lola could carry on with this kind of nonsense all the way to school but as Michael screeched into a sharp right hand bend, Lola had the perfect view of what happened next.

The final cage, full of younger children, suddenly broke loose and hurtled down a side road to the left, it was the road to the local sewage farm, where all the towns' toilet flushes ended up. The children had christened the road Plop Street.

Lola wasted no time...

"I think that I should raise the alarm, raise the alarm, raise the alarm, the little kids are heading to the sewage farm, sewage farm, sewage farm..."

"...Oh no, what are we gonna do? Are we gonna do? Are we gonna do?"

"The little kids are gonna be swimming in poo, swimming in poo, swimming in poo..."

Lola had the perfect view as the runaway cage, smashed through the gates of the poo factory, hit the curb and the kids and bags aboard flew through the air and landed in a huge pool of liquidised poop.

"...I can tell you, I can see from here, see from here, see from here..."

"The kids have landed in some diarrhoea, diarrhoea, diarrhoea..."

Luckily, all the kids and their bags were fished out by the sewage staff (or the poo people as they were known) and after a thorough disinfecting, no harm was done, but this obviously spelt the end for the baggage bus.

Immediately, Mr X was given some emergency funding to hire a proper school bus in the short term until a more permanent solution could be found. Although, it had to be done, Mr X was saddened because he was hoping that money may one day go to the school library. The library was perfect in every way apart from the fact that he had forgotten to order any books for it. Mr Dijon was also saddened as he was hoping the money would go to upgrading his Jacuzzi at his country chateau.

The next day the kids were really down having lost their baggage bus, so to cheer them up, Mr Bell held an impromptu Wednesday Waffle, even though it was only Tuesday.

They had already covered what happened on the bus, what are the worst liquids to go swimming in and in a completely unrelated story how the flights from the local airport were all now running on time again.

Oscar had managed to get the discussion back onto his favourite subject.

"Anyway, when we returned from holiday, Speedy, my pet tortoise was dead and his body was really stiff."

"That's what happens to dead bodies, it's called rigor mortis," Jack announced.

"So, my tortoise had rigor mortis?"

"I saw that too, with one of those dolphin things that was washed up on the beach," said Alan.

"Do you mean a porpoise?" asked Lucy.

"Yes, it was a porpoise with rigor mortis, and it was slightly yellow."

"Your porpoise with rigor mortis was probably suffering from jaundice," said Tim.

"Beautiful animal the porpoise, really gorgeous even if it had jaundice and rigor mortis," Chloe announced.

"Was it big?" asked Malcolm.

"Enormous."

"So, the gorgeous, enormous porpoise had jaundice and rigor mortis?" asked Lina.

"I have heard that if you eat a gorgeous, enormous porpoise with jaundice and rigor mortis, it could lead to baldness," said Dave earnestly.

"Let's ask Mr X! Erm...I mean sixty-seven," muttered Fred.

Mr Bell had been in a bit of a daydream during the last few minutes but he realised he had to stop the waffle pretty soon, as he had a very important lesson to teach about rhyming words and he was sure the class would find it very difficult.

Just then there was a knock on the door and Miss Andrews the secretary teetered in but she just stood at the doorway.

"Well?" asked Mr Bell

"I'm fine thank you," she replied.

"No, can I help you Miss Andrews?"

"Yes, Mr X told me to tell you that there will be an emergency meeting in the staff room at lunch time."

"About?"

"About an hour."

"No, what is the meeting about?"

"Fund raising."

"Oh no, not again," muttered Mr Bell.

So, a bit later on, Mr Bell entered the staff room and reluctantly took his seat for the meeting. Mr X sat at the head of the table, with Miss Andrews sitting next to him. Most of the other teachers were there too, checking their phones or checking children's exercise books, mainly checking their phones.

They included Mr Ree and Miss James. Mr Ree was new to the school as he had taken over from Mr Grimshaw. He kept himself to himself and no one really knew too much about him.

Miss James taught the youngest children in the school. She was quite young but had taught at Sandy Primary for three or four years. She had a reputation for being a bit of a party animal at the weekend and rather lazy during the week.

She always volunteered to do playtime duty, and initially Mr X thought she was a really hard worker. However, all was not as it seemed. She would sit on a chair in the shade and she encouraged the children to take it in turns to practice their massaging skills on her shoulders. Usually, this would result in Miss James falling asleep. The first time this happened, the children were too scared to wake her and the young kids had to teach themselves for the rest of the day. Strangely, it was their most productive afternoon. After that a special monitor was appointed to make sure she was awake when break ended.

"Thanks for coming everyone, as you know we can't keep the school bus going for long, so we need to brainstorm some ideas to fund raise money to buy a new one. Now we just want ideas, call things out and we can discuss them," Mr X announced.

Mr Bell shook his head despondently. Sandy Primary had had a pretty dismal record in fund raising in the past and he knew he would have to poo-poo the ideas that the teachers came up with.

"Sponsored walk?" asked one teacher

"Last time we lost twelve children," Mr Bell answered.

"Bake sale?"

"Salmonella poisoning last time."

"A quiz night?" asked Miss James.

"Don't you remember we tried that? Mr Grimshaw was in charge, we got a big cash prize and the plan was to sell lots of tickets for the quiz and make tonnes of money. Weirdly Mr Grimshaw forgot to tell anyone and he only sold one ticket."

"Who too?"

"His wife. She won and took the money, the school lost a fortune."

"Yes, that was unfortunate," Mr X interjected, "What about a sponsored swim?"

"We can't do that because of Dave."

"Remind me?"

Mr Bell sighed, "Dave is the most disorganised child that has ever lived," nods of agreement around the table as Mr Bell continued. "A couple of years ago, there was a big mix up with his bags. We had a fancy-dress day followed the next day by the sponsored swim. For the fancy dress, he came to school with the wrong bag and just wore a pair of swimming trunks."

"Oh yes, I remember, I thought he had come as an Olympic swimmer."

"No, the next day was the Sponsored swim at the local pool and Dave again brought the wrong bag. This time he bought his fancy dress clothes which were a medieval knight's costume complete with real chain mail."

"Cool!" said one of the teachers.

"No, not cool, he jumped straight in the pool and because his suit was so heavy he nearly drowned, the entire swimming pool staff had to jump in and save him and we got banned from ever using the pool again."

Mr Ree who as usual had been very quiet in the meeting looked up briefly and mumbled, "We should have a school fair."

Everyone was silent, they looked at each other. Mr Bell was thinking of some disaster from the past but couldn't, the school had never had a fair before. It was a great idea.

The group thrashed out ideas and decided on a fair just before the Christmas break. That gave them four or five weeks to get prepared. There would be food, drinks, lots of games and activities for the kids and even a visit from Santa.

Mr X had asked for a volunteer to coordinate the whole event. Just as he had, Miss James jolted herself awake (she had missed her daily snooze and nodded off in the meeting) making a strange noise as she did. It sounded a bit like 'me', she had also inadvertently thrown her hands up at the same time. Mr X saw this as a sign that she was really keen to get involved, so he gave her the title of Fair Coordinator.

With everything decided, an eager Fair Coordinator in place and plenty of time to plan the event, what could possibly go wrong?

In Sandy Primary School, pretty much everything!

The School Fair

Mr Bell knocked on Mr X's office door.

"Who is it?"

"You can see who it is, this is a glass door."

"Use it please."

"This is ridiculous and demeans us both."

"Do it!"

Mr Bell screwed his face up in frustration, and then he reached up. There was a small bell on the top right-hand side of the door. He flicked it.

"Ding."

"Miss Andrews, bell's gone," squeaked Mr X.

"No, Mr X, he is standing outside," Miss Andrews replied in a monotone manner, this was well-rehearsed routine.

This was the signal for Mr Bell to walk in. Mr Bell gave a fake belly laugh whilst putting his hands on his sides. Mr X was genuinely laughing his head off. This wasn't quite as good as when Dr Hoo came calling but he still found it amusing.

"This is stupid, I reckon you should reward me for removing that daft bell," Mr Bell said through gritted teeth.

"Do you mean give you a prize, for having no bell?"

"Yes, I should be rewarded with a no bell prize that should keep the peace around here. You should give me a Nobel peace prize!"

"Don't be silly Mr Bell, have you just come up here wasting my time with terrible jokes?" He reached in his jacket pocket for some tasty treats and leaned back in his chair.

"No, I came up here because I am not sleeping well…I am very worried about the school fair."

It had been a couple of weeks since the fund-raising meeting. Mr Bell loved to be involved in school events but had been given a back seat because Miss James was so keen to volunteer for the coordinator's role. He found that hard to swallow, but he was really worried as he knew what Miss James was like, she tended to leave everything to the last minute.

"Everything is under control, I sent the letters to all the parents last week, it's on the website, everyone knows about it and it's even in the local paper."

"No, that side of it is great, should be a huge turnout, I mean do you think Miss James is capable of getting everything ready?"

"This is exactly what she needs, she was so enthusiastic in the meeting and I think this will be the making of her…"

"But…"

"But…we should not butt in, she is more than capable, let her work through the details, just relax Mr Bell."

"Can I at least organise the fake Santa?"

"Do you really want to?"

"Oh yeah, I love all that, my friend has a costume, the coat, the beard, the wig, so much fun…erm not that wigs are fun of course."

"I wouldn't know," replied Mr X sarcastically whilst reaching for more calming snacks. "Very well, but you and I will not be dressing up as Santa, we need to be chatting with the parents."

As Mr Bell returned to his classroom, he felt relieved that he had something to concentrate on and maybe Mr X was right about Miss James. Suddenly, he heard a strange, low pitch sound. He peered over the balcony, it was half way through break time. He scanned the playground to spy Miss James snoring her head off in the corner. His anxiety instantly returned.

"So, everyone, remember tomorrow is the big day, I hope you can all make it, you may even see Santa!" It was a Friday afternoon, the day before the school fair and Mr Bell was drumming up some final support for the event.

"Is the real Santa coming?" asked Bob.

"No Bob, he only comes on the twenty fifth."

"Three times seven."

"Nice try Fred. No Bob, he only comes on Christmas Day, this will be a fake one, but you can use your imagination, and you can get a photo with him. And before you ask, I will not be the fake Santa!"

"Yes, he's not quite fat enough," whispered Jack to Malcolm. Malcolm laughed and trumped at the same time.

"Is Santa going to lose his home?" inquired one of the twins.

"What do you mean?" replied Mr Bell, final cup of tea of the week in his hand.

"Well I read about Global Warming, the world is getting hotter and the polar bears are going to melt."

"No Kath, I mean Kim, the polar bears won't melt but the polar ice-caps might, then there could be floods and the polar bears will lose their habitat."

"So, Santa will lose his home, I was right."

"There are those new houses on the High Street, maybe Santa could move into one of them," announced Lucy. All the children nodded their heads in agreement.

"It would be more convenient for him for sure," Mr Bell concluded.

"My mum says global warming is caused by natural gas, so technically every time you fart, you are killing a polar bear," Kyle announced confidently.

All eyes immediately turned to Malcolm and his trumpy trousers, who was just lifting his bottom to let another one slide out.

"Technically, your mum is right, but if that was the case Malcolm would have killed half the planet by now," Mr Bell replied chuckling. Malcolm laughed too and another guff popped out of his trumpy trousers, only adding to the Global crisis.

"Blimey, his gas-pipes are leaking again, that's not afternoonified!" cried Hettie.[6]

"Mr Bell, are you sure everything will be ready for tomorrow? It's just I know Miss James is running everything," said Chloe.

"Of course, Chloe, why would you ask that?" Mr Bell's temple began to throb.

"Well, when she's not asleep, she seems to be in the pub. My dad has seen her in the boozer every night this week."

"The fair starts at eleven in the morning, the teachers will all be there at nine to help Miss James set things up. She assured me earlier, everything is under control." Mr Bell had to hold onto his desk, he suddenly felt a bit dizzy.

Mr Bell didn't sleep a wink that night, and he was the first one at the school the next day.

"It's nine thirty, where the heck is she?" Mr Bell cried whilst pacing up and down the playground.

"Her car is pulling up now," shouted Miss Andrews who was scanning the horizon for signs of the fair coordinator.

Miss James entered the school gates, she looked slightly wobbly and was wearing a huge pair of sunglasses.

"What time do you call this and where is all the stuff for the fair?" screamed Mr Bell.

"Please don't shout I have a terrible hangov...headache, it's all under control."

"Okay, okay, Miss James had a budget and plenty of time to prepare for the fair, let's go through each item and take things from there," Mr X said calmly. "First up, food?"

"Yes, yes, lots of burgers and sausages for the barbeque."

"Great, well done for bringing the barbeque with you, that's something else the school should invest in."

6   There will be a full list of Hettie's Victorian phrases at the end of the book, so everything will be bang up to the elephant.

"Do you mean we don't have an actual barbeque to cook them on?" replied Miss James. "Oh dear."

"Surely that's something the fair coordinator would have checked!" Mr Bell bellowed. "What about games?"

"Oh dear, forgot about them!"

"Face paints?"

"Now they were definitely on my list, but I forgot to buy them. But I have got sponges for sponge the teacher, well not sponges exactly but small rubbery, spongy type balls."

"Are you sure they are suitable?" asked Mr X.

"They will be fine, and we got loads of toys donated by Dave's dad," Miss James responded trying to deflect the attention away from the untested, potentially unsafe sponge the teacher equipment.

"Drinks?"

"Absolutely, got a great deal at the local pub, got gallons of wine and beer for the parents and loads of fizzy drinks for the kids!"

"So essentially, if I have got this correct, your plan is to let the parents get drunk, let the kids get hyper on sugar, give them no food or entertainment and then let them throw things at us. There is going to be a riot!" screamed Mr Bell who was beginning to hyperventilate.

"Well at least we have music," chuckled Mr X.

"Oh, the stereo and speakers! I knew I'd forgotten something."

"Forgotten everything!" cried Mr Bell.

Mr X took charge, "Okay, okay. Here is the plan. Mr Bell, needs a cup of tea, then as usual he will come up with a master plan to get us out of this fairly big fair mess. Miss Andrews to the kettle, everyone else to Miss James' car to unload the drinks, the food we can't cook, the kind of sponges and donated toys!"

After several calming teas for Mr Bell, calming snacks for Mr X and a quick power nap from the fair coordinator, a plan was hatched, just as the first visitors arrived.

A bar was set up in the Games Room. Miss James had certainly gone to town with the drinks, there was every choice you could think of. Kids could drink and play games whilst the parents could just drink. A 'sponge the teacher' area was set up in Miss Jones' favourite dozing spot and the gates were opened so that everyone could wander onto the beach. Mr Bell's plan was to keep everyone well refreshed for an hour or so before he would unleash his secret weapon. Santa.

The toys that were donated could be used as gifts for Santa to hand out and the school could make some money by charging for a photo with Father Christmas. The only issue was to find someone who could fill Santa's boots but Mr Bell had a victim, sorry a volunteer in mind. And he had just entered the school.

"Mark, how are you doing mate?"

"Now then Mr Bell, I can tell you want something, you always want something."

"Not at all, in fact I wanted to buy my favourite parent a drink," Mr Bell ushered Mark into the Games Room. Mark was Lucy's dad and was a great parent, always ready to help. Mr Bell knew he would make a perfect Santa, due to his friendly nature, more importantly, due to his enormous belly. He knew how to persuade him too; a few beers should do the trick.

"Miss Andrews, please give Mark anything he wants, all on me."

Mr Bell was about to broach the subject of Santa with Mark but he scanned the room and saw trouble brewing. The parents were really going for the cheap booze and the kids were going into crazy-mode with the endless supply of sugar close by. The pool table had already been broken and some of the kids were arguing.

Time for some distraction, sponge the teacher would be perfect, Miss James had set it up but had not announced anything so it was time to strike.

"Ladies and gentlemen, boys and girls, let's all go outside for the sponge the teacher, first teacher up is...Mr Ree," Mr Bell announced just as Mr Ree walked in. Cheers and claps and most of the throng headed outside. Mr Ree looked confused, and slightly scared as the mob shepherded him over to the hot seat.

The sponging area was ready, Miss James to her credit had marked out a line where the kids could throw from, although it was rather close to where the teachers were going to sit. Miss James' boyfriend who arrived just as the fair began, had also managed to find some scrap wood and quickly made what looked like an old-fashioned set of stocks. The teacher sat down and could put their head through a hole in the wood, whilst the kids took aim.

A huge queue had formed and at the head of it stood Bob. Bob wasn't the most academic child, but he was the school star when it came to sports. He had a great shot and a great aim. He slowly dunked the first ball into the bucket of water and prepared to fire. The ball absorbed the water and instead of going soft, turned into a solid mass that felt more like a stone.

Even Bob knew this could be dangerous but the baying crowd forced him to throw. "Throw it, throw it, throw it!" they jeered.

Bob looked around, gulped and then he threw the ball, it flew like a rocket right into Mr Ree's nose. Time seemed to stand still but a few seconds later, Mr Ree's nose, just appeared to explode, there was blood everywhere. If Mr Bell needed a Rudolf to go with his Santa, Mr Ree would have been perfect. Mr Ree tried to stand up but just as he did he whacked the back of his head on the stocks and passed out while still sitting in the chair.

Silence. Absolute silence.

"Is he dead?" Oscar enquired hopefully. This was followed by a massive cheer of, "Again, again!"

Mr X took control and decided this would be a perfect time for a welcome speech which included a reminder about safety and why everyone was here today, to avoid any more accidents within the school. Meanwhile, Miss Andrews called an ambulance.

As Mr Ree was being carried out, Mr Bell re-entered the Games Room and found Mark in a very happy mood. So, after another beer, all was agreed and as things looked like they could turn nasty pretty soon (the school was now completely full of children and parents), the plan was to meet in the car-park in five minutes where Mark could get changed and bring in the toys for the children.

Mr Bell ran to his room where he had the toys ready in two large black bin bags, he grabbed them along with the Santa suit. He sneaked out the back door and waited for Mark next to Miss James' car.

Mark wobbled over a minute or two later, he had certainly made the most of the bar and his ruddy checks would be perfect for the role. As he tried to get the suit on, both men realised that it wouldn't fit over his shirt and jeans.

"Oh, the heck with it, I'll just take my clothes off," and with that Mark stripped down to his underpants and put the suit on top. It was still a very tight fit and his very hairy chest was clearly visible where the costume was stretching to the limit. With beard and hat in place, everything was ready. Mr Bell had even remembered the school bell (Mr Bell had bought a new one, as a Christmas present to the school), so Santa could ring it as he entered the gates.

Now in the time Mr Bell had gone away, things had really turned ugly, all the drinks had gone and the hungry horde had started to look for someone to blame. Mr X had bravely locked himself in his office and most of the other teachers had escaped along the beach. The kids had started a chant of, "We want Santa, we want Santa!" Miss James had started a separate chant of, "We want more beer!"

Mr Bell was leading Santa down the path and towards the gate, when he got there, he planned to announced Santa's arrival and organise a sensible way to distribute the toys.

"Now everyone, we have a special guest all the way from the North Pole, let's give a big welcome to..."

"Let's get the toys!"

"Attack Santa, it's not the real one, it's only Lucy's dad!"

"More beer!"

"Attack Santa!"

"Fifty-four!" screamed Fred.

With that the children attacked, Mr Bell was knocked down in the stampede. "Santa is very tired please form an orderly queue," were his last words before he disappeared under the children's feet.

Santa was grabbed from all angles, instantly his suit was ripped and Mark's hairy belly and chest were on show. Next his red trousers went, and finally someone stole his hat and wig. The bags too were ripped apart and the booty shared out amongst the marauding mob. When the chaos had calmed, Mark stood frozen in just a Santa beard (twisted over his head) and a pair of underpants, holding a bell in his right hand. He looked a little bit like a strange, chubby tribute to the Statue of Liberty.

Even more strangely, a couple of people paid for photographs with him but this was not the money-making scheme that the school had hoped for. When the money was tallied up the following week, Sandy Primary had actually lost money and they were no closer to getting a school bus.

Luckily, Kath and Kim's dad again came to the rescue. Being a pilot he said he could get his hands on an old mobile staircase used for passengers to get off aeroplanes[7]. He thought it would make a fabulous school bus, although the kids would have to duck when in any tunnels. Michael was again at the helm, and it was a complete hit with the kids.

---

7   In a completely unrelated incident, forty-seven people broke their legs when then tried to step off an Easy-Tiger flight at the local airport only to find someone had stolen the staircase.

Sports Day

"So, children, I am afraid Rock, Paper, Scissors will have to be added to the list of banned games in the playground. I have reports that real rocks, paper and scissors have been used. Rocks and scissors I feel could be dangerous and the chance of a paper cut doesn't bear thinking about."

It was Wednesday morning and Mr X was in front of the school conducting another assembly. "Since we have our new teachers here, Mr Bell this may be a good time to remind everyone of the full list of banned games."

After the recent fair fiasco, Miss James had been fired (she had since left teaching and landed a dream position of a hammock tester) and Mr Ree was too traumatised to return to Sandy Primary. They had been replaced by Miss Snow and Miss Tree. Miss Snow had taken over the infants and had substituted in the school before, so everyone already knew her. Miss Tree was new, and no one knew anything about her. They had already been introduced to the children and were standing at the front of the assembly room.

"Certainly Mr X, the full list is as follows," Mr Bell took a piece of paper from his pocket. "Ultimate tag, off-ground tag, normal tag, abnormal tag, bunnies, killer, killer bunnies, killer bunnies two, fluffy bunnies, killer fluffy bunnies, stop the oxygen, sumo squash, bulldog, ultimate bulldog, bull, bulls, dog, dogs, killer dogs, killer frogs, kings, queens, aces, hopper, hopper two, what's the time Mr Pyscho?, Jack's house of pain, kiss chase, punch chase, kick chase, pinch chase, basket case, suitcase, piley on, dude, where's my hat?, tsunami alert, do infants bounce?, kicker, kicker two, limb-breaker, fruit salad, fruit crusher, dodge ball, dodge hat, dodge rock, dodge stick, dodge punch, dodge bullet, Dodge Wars, Star Wars, World Wars, drunken tag, nausea drunken tag, spin, vomit, spin vomit, vomit spin, The Living Dead versions one to eighteen, killer

hopscotch, fluffy hopscotch, killer fluffy pyscho abnormal ultimate hopscotch one and two and finally Rock, Paper, Scissors."

"Excellent, so we don't expect to hear that anyone has been playing any of these dangerous games ever again," Mr X confirmed confidently. He was right too, the children wouldn't, they would dream up some even more dangerous and violent ways to pass the time.

"That brings us to our weekly *some people* session, who would like to begin?"

Mr X had dreamt up a clever and devious way for the children to tell tales on each other. The children would take turns saying 'some people have or haven't been' and then describe which rule they had broken. The children thought this was a safe way to tell on their friends without giving away the culprits' names. In reality, the teachers could tell instantly by the guilty looks on the kids' faces who the wrongdoers were. As usual Chloe was the first one with her hand up.

"Yes, Chloe."

"Some people haven't been wearing hats," Chloe announced.

"Well we know that no hat means no play, and in this hot weather, a lack of hat could lead to some serious sun burn."

All eyes instantly turned towards Oscar who had a big red sunburnt face. His beetroot cheeks, if possible, seemed to glow even more as everyone stared at him.

"Yes Alan?"

"Some people have been painting without using Art t-shirts."

"Well, that is not a good idea, as it can ruin a very expensive uniform."

This time everyone turned towards the twins who were covered in a multi-coloured array of poster paints. Their rainbow faces seemed to turn redder on the spectrum.

"Some people have not been aiming very well when they go to the toilet."

This was a regular on the *some people* forum and instead of looking for one remorseful face, every single boy, including Tim who had brought up the subject, looked sheepish and guilt-ridden.

"At Sandy Primary, we aim to please, can the boys aim too, please!" This was Mr X's usual response and he chuckled to himself.

The session continued with more tales of running on the balconies, illegal games room vouchers, reading when they shouldn't, sliding down the bannister of the new school bus, untidy desks and pretending to be from the Victorian era. Finally, someone mentioned the subject Mr X had been waiting for.

"Some people have been eating shiny packets."

Mr X was obsessed with healthy snacks and realised from experience how easy it was to get into bad habits by eating snacks like crisps, crackers and other salty products. He still kept healthy options in his pocket but had never eaten a raisin since the guinea-pig mix up. He had asked the caretaker, Mr Foy to fish out all the empty shiny packets from the bins from the previous week and he picked up an enormous black bin bag that was at the front of the assembly room.

"This is one weeks' worth of junk," he said and emptied the bin bag all over the floor. There were gasps from the kids at the scale of the shiny problem that the school had.

"Sometimes we are known as SPS for short, yesterday in town I heard some kids from another school saying that stood for Seriously Porky Students. I think we need to go on a health kick."

"We are not that bad," Malcolm interrupted, as he did he let off an enormous fart that pushed himself forward, bursting two of the buttons on his shirt that propelled through the air and hit Mr X on the face.

"Some people are in denial Malcolm...I don't mean the river in Egypt, I mean they can't see they have a problem, so from now on, all shiny packets are banned from the school, only healthy snacks are allowed," Mr X stated calmly whilst handing back Malcolm's buttons. There were groans and moans from the children.

"Mr X, my mum makes my packed lunches in advance, tomorrow I have an apple in a shiny packet, is that okay?" Jack inquired.

"An apple in a shiny packet?" Mr X repeated suspiciously. "I guess that's okay."

"Well it's apple slices really."

"Still fine, I suppose."

"Well when I say apple, it's actually potato slices."

"Plain boiled slices of potatoes, could be a healthy choice."

"Well they are more like fried crisp shaped potatoes, not really plain, more in a salt and vinegar style."

"So, you mean a bag of salt and vinegar crisps Jack?"

"Yes, I guess essentially that's what it is, still okay?"

"No Jack, not okay. Okay?"

"Okay."

"Good, and a final announcement, to help with our health drive, Sandy Primary is going to hold its first ever proper Sports Day!"

Silence. Absolute Silence.

"Can't we just have the fun day on the beach like we always do? Please?" pleaded Lucy theatrically.

"Please?" pleaded Alan.

"Please?" pleaded Dave.

"Please?" pleaded Lina.

"Thirty-seven?" pleaded Fred.

"No children, for two reasons. Firstly, as last year, about three quarters of you didn't actually do any exercise, you just spent your time at the beach store buying junk. And the second reason is because of what happened to Mrs Thomas. Mr Bell, could you remind us of the details please."

Mr Bell had been sitting in the corner, drinking tea and updating the banned games list, he stood up and addressed the audience. "Mrs Thomas was our old music teacher, really, literally old, it was her last day before she retired. She had never taken part in the teachers' race before, so we helped her out of her wheel chair and steadied her for the race."

"And?" Mr X interjected.

"And, some people had decided that it would be funny to dig a huge hole in the sand where the teachers were due to race, cover the hole with sticks and leaves and basically make a bear trap for teachers. It was like slow motion, sorry it was slow motion as Mrs Thomas shuffled her way down the sand, she had never looked happier, time stood still as she plummeted, incredibly slowly into the hole. She broke every bone in her body, and will never play the violin again. To be fair, she wasn't that good at the fiddle before the accident, but that's not the point. It was completely irresponsible. We never did find out who dug that hole."

All eyes slowly turned towards Jack and Malcolm.

"So, this year," Mr X took over. "We have hired the football pitch in the town, no chance of a teacher bear trap this year. We are going to have proper races, singing and chanting, and it will be a great advert for our new healthy, happy school. The local newspaper will be there, Mr Dijon, the school owner, has cancelled a cruise to be present and I am going to invite the mayor. Since this is Sandy Primary School, it's bound to be a rip-roaring success."

"We have six weeks to get ready, we don't need *some people*, we just need one person to take responsibility for the whole event."

All eyes slowly moved to focus on one man who had a throbbing temple and desperately needed another cup of tea.

So, the whole event was left in the capable hands of Mr Bell to organise. After several sleepless nights and several hundred cups of tea, a plan was hatched. As there were about one hundred children in the school, he decided to split them into twelve teams with about eight kids in each team. The teams would be named after the animals in the Chinese New Year Calendar (a TV programme had popped up at four in the morning when Mr Bell couldn't sleep, all about the story of the animals crossing a river and in his sleep-deprived state, it seemed like a perfectly logical idea), and each team would wear different colours too. This worked well for the Red Dragons, Pink Pigs, White Rams and Green Snakes but Mr Bell ran out of colours so ended up with Purple Rabbits, Blue Dogs and Orange Roosters. He thought he could explain this by saying it was to do with genetically modified species and cloning.

Each class would race and earn points for their teams. The races would consist of all the classics: running, bean bag on head, egg and spoon, three-legged; and would culminate in a team relay. He ordered some trophies and medals and Miss Snow and Miss Tree could make posters and flags for all the teams. The children could practice two or three times a week for the events and of course, Mr X wanted some singing and chanting too.

All the typical chants like, *Oggie, Oggie, Oggie, There was a Fly* and a version of *Who Let the Dogs Out?* Would be fun and easy enough to teach. Mr Bell even wrote a special chant for the school that went like this:

We are the children from Sandy School,

We take a pride in the things we do,

Working together and having fun,

Who's for a Sports Day?

Everyone! (All the kids jump in the air)

So, over the next few weeks, the kids practiced and really seemed to enjoy the whole idea of exercising, chanting and being part of a team. The day before the big day, everyone was really excited and everything had gone exactly to plan.

Mr Bell was worried. Really worried.

Mr X saw him outside his office and realised this wasn't the time for the silly doorbell nonsense, so he went outside to talk to him.

"Mr Bell, chin up, everything has gone fantastically, I am very proud of your hard work and the children are so excited. Mr Foy says he hasn't found a shiny packet in the bin for weeks, and look at the children at lunchtime, practicing the races, not killing each other. Even Jack is excited, he has been practicing the chanting with the little kids, it's all positive."

"That's the problem, everything is perfect, that never happens at Sandy Primary, something is bound to go wrong," Mr Bell replied shaking his head.

"Tish and tosh, remember the six Ps."

"Pardon?"

"Perfect planning prevents poor performance."

"That's only five Ps."

"Oh yes, the last one is...probably, as you know some factors are out of our control. The worst thing that could happen tomorrow is if it rains, nothing we can do about that, you have done a great job, I can't see anything else going wrong! Just relax Mr Bell tomorrow will be a day that will be remembered forever."

As Mr Bell returned to his class, he felt reassured, the children had responded to the health drive, Mr X was right, maybe he was worrying for nothing. It was almost time to go home, so he would use the last few minutes to drum up even more enthusiasm for the big day.

"Mr Bell, I am in the dogs' team, can I bring Jabba to Sports Day tomorrow?"

"Who is Jabba, Dave?"

"My pet dog, Jabba the Mutt. He is very friendly."

"Sure, why not!"

"My mum says we shouldn't be doing these silly races, we should do the events that are performed in the Olympics. She should know, she used to be an Olympic athlete," Kyle proudly announced.

Mr Bell didn't want the negative vibes from Kyle to spoil the mood and dampen the excitement, so he thought it was time to put him in his place. "Look Kyle, we are all a bit bored of thoughts from your mum, she wasn't in the Olympics, don't tell tales, and if your mum has anything else to say to me, tell her to talk to me face-to-face. Understood?"

Some of the children giggled and Kyle scowled back at Mr Bell.

"Tomorrow is going to be fantastic, the worst thing that can happen is if it rains! Off you go, don't be late in the morning."

The next morning when Mr Bell opened his curtains, it was the most glorious sunny day.

"Morning Mr Bell, magnificent day, the colours of the teams are fantastic and the flags and posters are amazing. The newspaper reporter is in a cab along with Mr and Mrs Dijon and the mayor is already here. This is going to be a memorable day all round!" with that Mr X thrust a radio microphone into Mr Bell's hand and gave him the thumbs up to start the event. He then rushed off to sit next to the mayor.

Mr Bell introduced the teams and each one paraded around the pitch, waving and cheering just like an Olympic Opening Ceremony.

Mr Bell began to relax into his role and started cracking terrible jokes about each team such as: Hop to it rabbits, hey horses why the long faces? And you won't have a leg to stand on if you cheat snakes. The first set of running races all went to plan and next up was the egg and spoon race. Mr Bell spied the reporter taking his seat in the stand next to Mr X, the mayor and the Dijons.

When it came to Mr Bell's class to race, as usual Bob was favourite to win, he had just stormed in first in the running race. His parents were so pumped up for the race and they were yelling and screaming for a repeat performance. Out of the corner of his eye, Mr Bell noticed Chloe's dad giving her some last-minute instructions, and he was pretty sure he handed something to his daughter. When the whistle went, it wasn't Bob but Chloe who charged out in front, the egg (actually a golf ball) didn't move a hair's breadth whilst all the other kids, including Bob kept dropping theirs. In the end, Chloe won by miles, with Bob in second place. When she crossed the line, Chloe waved at her dad and turned the egg upside down, it still didn't move, it was stuck firmly in the spoon. Bob's dad spotted the underhand (or under egg) dirty dealings and erupted with rage.

"You cheated, she's got glue or Blutack under her egg!" Bob's dad screamed pointing a finger at Chloe.

"Hey calm down, calm down, and don't be ridiculous, there is no glue or Blutack," Chloe's dad replied. "She won fair and square, you take things too seriously, look at you, you are in full running gear, just to win the parents race I guess...here, chill out and have a chewing gum," with that Chloe's dad offered him a pellet and winked.

"Chewing gum, I knew it, you're cheating…" Bob's dad aimed a punch at Chloe's dad.

"Hey, leave him alone!" screamed Chloe's mum and she jumped on Bob's dad's back.

"Get off my husband!" wailed Bob's mum and she entered the fray swinging her handbag as if it was Thor's deadly hammer.

Mr Bell tried to keep the warring factions apart and tried to use his hands to block the photographs from the newspaper reporter who had vacated his seat and had headed straight over to record the unexpected wrestling bout. Other parents had joined in on both sides of the contest and some of the sports equipment, like bean bags and batons, were being hurled about.

Lucy's dad, Mark, had only just finished therapy for the Santa attack and suddenly he found himself in the middle of another violent incident. Weirdly, a few minutes later, he had again been stripped down to his undies and was left standing, dumbstruck with a cone on his head in the middle of the pitch. He really needed a break from school events he thought to himself.

Worse was to come. Mr Bell extracted himself from the ongoing tussle to see Kyle approaching him, striding confidently, next to the largest, most muscular woman Mr Bell had ever seen.

"Ah Mr Bell, I don't think you have ever met my mum, have you? You said you would like to talk to her face to face."

Mr Bell gulped, shook his head and strained his neck up to see the face of the colossal woman now standing inches away from him. Kyle's mum grabbed Mr Bell by the lapels and lifted him up, for what seemed like an eternity, until their faces were almost touching. Mr Bell's legs dangled down like two hairy wind chimes, somewhere near the giantess' midriff.

"I, Kyle's mother. I hear you disrespect him and I. I represent the Soviet Union at three Olympic Games. You know which sports Missta Bell?" Mr Bell just squeaked. "Wrestling and shot put." With that she chucked Mr Bell towards where the teams were sitting, then pounced on him and put him in a head lock. Mr Bell's face went a funny colour and his vision was beginning to fade, this wasn't helped by the flash of the reporter's camera that was documenting the action.

"Mr Bell is getting batty-fanged, someone help him!" screamed Hettie.

"Is he dead?" Oscar screamed hopefully.

The other teachers ran over and tried to pull Kyle's mum off the semi-conscious event organiser. Mr X looked at the shocked faces of his VIP guests and then surveyed the horrific scene of carnage on the pitch. Chloe's dad was squashing chewing gum into Bob's dad's hair and Bob's mum was trying to stuff a bean-bag into Chloe's mum's mouth. Mark was still practically naked and was sobbing. Time for some diversionary tactics he thought.

"Chanting, start the chanting!" he bellowed at no one in particular.

"Am all over it Mr X!" shouted Jack and he jumped up and positioned himself in front of the teams.

"Oggie, oggie, oggie!" Jack chanted.

"Oi, oi, oi!" the kids replied instantly.

"Alright gang, just as we have practiced, let's perform Mr Bell's special chant!"

The children all stood to attention and with perfect timing chanted:

We are the children of the porky school,

We hate fruit and veggies and exercise too,

Surfing the Internet and sitting on our bum,

Who's for some junk food?

Everyone! (All the children jumped in the air)

At the same time, Malcolm and Jack suddenly produced two huge black bin bags and threw the contents up into the air. They were full of empty and half-empty shiny packets. The boys had not only been teaching the other children a different version of the chant, they had also been collecting all the shiny packets that the children had still been eating at school, before Mr Foy could find them in the bin.

As soon as they began floating to the floor, Jabba the Mutt, who had been sitting calming watching the action, sprung up and began hoovering up all the scraps from the crisps and other snacks.

"We don't want exercise, we want extra fries, to the tuck shop comrades!" Jack commanded, and the teams flooded out of the arena, following their Leader in Lardiness.

The mayor had seen enough of the chaos and was heading for the exit too, when Jabba ran in front of him and evacuated his bowels of all the salty rubbish he had just gobbled down. The mayor had no time to change direction and he slipped up in Jabba's massive plop and landed right next to the half dead Mr Bell and some battle-weary parents. Mr X's wig had nearly committed suicide in shock and the Dijons had turned a very pale colour. Shiny packets blew in the breeze all around them. It made a great photograph for the reporter, who couldn't believe his luck at the sports-day-turned- massacre, he had been sent to cover.

As Mr Bell squinted through his scratched and bent glasses at the newspaper from his hospital bed the next day, the photo was pride of place. The headline read: Sandy's Shambolic and Shiny Sports Day.

Oh well, this would certainly be a day everyone would remember and at least it didn't rain!

Is Honesty the Best Policy?

"He's definitely alive, my mum saw him in town yesterday, he had a big scraggly beard and long hair but it was him."

"But that's impossible, he was killed in the hurricane, he was at school when it hit."

"He's dead for sure," Oscar confirmed.

It was a Wednesday morning, just before nine o'clock and a huge rumour buzz had taken over the school. The children had huddled together in the playground discussing Kyle's extraordinary breaking news, the gossip that Mr Grimshaw was actually still alive.

"My mum knows what happened, her friend whatsapped her yesterday, apparently on the day of the storm, he slipped away from school, in the school bus, robbed the town's bank with his wife and hid the cash somewhere. He has now come back to collect the money," Kyle announced to the gathering of children eager to hear. Kyle was in his element, and after the Sports Day, no one was too keen to say his mum wasn't telling the truth.

"But we would have seen him leave, I remember seeing him at school that day, we all do, he was tidying up the Games Room that afternoon," Tim replied. As Tim was an expert on the Games Room, everyone nodded in agreement, that seemed to be everyone's memory of the day.

"I saw him leave."

Everyone froze and turned slowly towards the voice that spoke. It was Fred.

"What?" the kids all chorused.

"I saw him leave," Fred repeated calmly.

"But why didn't you say anything?" screamed Oscar.

"Because nobody asked."

During the fateful day as everyone was paying attention to the evacuation advice of the teachers, Fred as usual had been in his happy place of not paying any attention. He had been daydreaming but as he stared out of the window, he spotted Mr Grimshaw making a hasty exit in the school bus just before the end of the day.

"What time was this Fred? It's very important we know," Kyle quizzed Fred quite forcefully, and suddenly Fred felt pressured and reverted to his usual uncommunicative self.

"What time Fred?" everyone screamed.

But Fred just shook his head. Ellie had been half reading, half listening but she knew how to extract an answer.

"Shh, everyone, you are asking Fred a direct maths question about time, I don't think he will answer," she put her book on the floor. "We need a different strategy, she winked to her friends. What did you all watch on TV last night?" The kids immediately picked up on the plan

"History Channel," said Tim.

"Dead Animals and how to dissect them," replied Oscar.

"Oliver Twist," answered Hettie.

"Chart Show," said Lola.

Fred heard the word watch so happily answered the question about time, "I saw Mr Grimshaw leave at exactly two minutes to three."

So, the children were all convinced that it was true and gossiped and gossiped until Chloe did her to bell impression (the bell had been stolen again) and they lined up ready for class. They were all now convinced Mr Grimshaw had had time to rob the bank and hide the money, he was alive and back in town.

Mr Bell and the other teachers had also talked of nothing else, Kyle had rushed up to Mr X's office to pass on Fred's exclusive revelation and it was decided to talk about it during the assembly later that morning.

So, after the children had come into class and calmed slightly, it was time for the Wednesday Waffle.

As the topic of Mr Grimshaw was on hold until later, and no one had brought anything special in to talk about, Mr Bell went over to the ideas jar. He had a plastic jar on his table that the children could put ideas of topics to talk about. He reached into the jar and held the paper up to his eyes. It looked like Jack's writing and it said 'How are babies made again?'

Mr Bell wasn't prepared for this one today, that would need a lot more tea consumption, so he made an executive decision to change the topic. "Okay, someone has written here that they would like to talk about honesty."

"Really, who wrote that Mr Bell?" Jack inquired suspiciously.

"Not sure, but it's an excellent topic," Mr Bell lied whilst crumpling up the paper in his hand. "Yes, it's incredibly important to always, on all occasions, tell the truth, I am so proud that someone wanted to discuss this very meaningful issue," Mr Bell fibbed to his impressionable class.

Just then, there was a knock on the door and Miss Andrews tottered in with a note in her hand.

"Ah Miss Andrews, always a pleasure when you disrupt our class," Mr Bell lied, although he was actually glad of the distraction today, to get him well away from the *where are babies from?* topic.

"I am very sorry to disturb you Mr Bell but I have a message for all the children from Mr X," Miss Andrews lied back. She actually loved interrupting the classes at Sandy Primary. It was her favourite part of the job, she would often linger outside listening for the right moment to enter, such as the time a teacher might say, this is very important, or in the middle of a test. It had become a little game to annoy the teachers, but today she had got her timing wrong.

"Mr X would like to remind you all that there is no running water today, the water company have said they have their best men on the job to fix it (another lie), but in the meantime, there is bottled water in the staffroom if you need to fill your water-bottles and we will put baby-wipes in the bathrooms, to clean your hands after you have used the toilet."

The children all groaned and Miss Andrews teetered away to annoy another teacher. Since no-one was really bothered to talk about the topic of telling the truth, Mr Bell decided to move on to his history lesson about World War Two.

"I'm sure you all remember, last week, we pretended to be evacuees and wrote letters and made photographs to send back to your parents as if it was 1942," Mr Bell held some examples up to show the class. "Although, Bob, I am pretty sure they didn't have mobile phones back then, and in your letter, you asked your mum who won *The X-Factor*…but…anyway…to make them look more old-fashioned, we are going to stain them with tea and even burn them around the edges."

"Cool!" most of the class responded. The tea wasn't a particular thrill, but the thought of something a bit more dangerous was.

Mr Bell held up some tea-bags and a couple of lighters. He then stressed to the class the importance of safety and that he would be the only one doing any of the burning. Again, there were groans from the class.

"Mr Bell, are the lighters from any of the teachers who smoke?" Lucy asked.

"Of course not, I don't know any teachers who smoke," he lied back, making a mental note to return the lighters back to Miss Tree and Miss Snow before break-time.

Mr Bell then took the class into the playground and set up an area outside, where one by one he could carefully burn the edges of the papers. The children could then dab wet tea over the paper, and so their work would look brown and charred, as if it had been discovered after an air-raid.

Mr Bell started with Alan's letter and the class gathered around to see his work go up in smoke. Mr Bell took great care to ensure there was no disaster, and just the perimeter of the paper was burnt away. Mr Bell had foolishly only taken one of the lighters outside, a fact that didn't escape Jack's eagle eyes. He gestured to Malcolm to sneak back into the classroom, which he duly did.

"What?"

"He's only burning a little bit, I reckon there would have been more damage in the war, let's burn our own letters," Jack whispered quietly while pointing at Mr Bell's desk where the second lighter stood.

After being inspired by Mr Bell's advice about telling the truth, it took Malcolm all of a millisecond to make the right decision, and it took the boys all of ten seconds to grab the lighter, and their letters and head to the boys' toilet.

Mr Bell and the rest of the class hadn't noticed that the two boys had disappeared, they were all too focused on fire and tea.

"Okay, we haven't got long, pass yours here, I will burn them all together," Jack ordered as they stood outside the cubicles, and Malcolm duly passed him his work. It took a few attempts, then suddenly the lighter burst into life and the papers ignited.

"We gotta be careful Jack, the smoke alarms, remember?"

"All under control," Jack replied cockily, just as the flames began engulfing the work, he instantly panicked and dropped them on the floor. "Water quick!" he screamed. Malcom tried the taps, but there was nothing coming out.

"The water's off, what we gonna do?" Malcolm was hyperventilating, he also farted at the same time which didn't help, particularly with flames so close. Jack surveyed the chaos and amazingly thought of a way out of this disaster.

"We're gonna have to wee on them!"

"What?"

"Wee!"

"Wee?"

"Wee!"

"Why?"

"We've got no water but we've got wee! It is the toilet, you are supposed to wee in the toilet!" Jack could see no other way and the papers had almost disappeared and the smoke was rising rapidly.

Malcolm was going to argue that you are supposed to wee in the actual toilet, not on your work which is on the floor, but Jack was right, incredibly, it was the only option.

We won't go into the exact details (the wee details if you are Scottish), but thirty seconds later, the flames were out and the smouldering remains of their work were in a soggy pile on the floor.

"We (or wee) shall never speak of this again," Jack declared. Malcolm was still in shock but managed to trump in agreement. The boys had avoided burning the school down and the smoke alarms going off but they still had to get back to class and ensure Mr Bell didn't discover the truth. They picked up the soggy, yellow papers gingerly, sneaked back into the classroom and put the lighter back in its rightful place.

Then they re-joined the class in the front playground with their wee-stained pieces of history in their hands. In all the excitement of burning their work, none of the children noticed the boys had been missing. Neither had Mr Bell, particularly as the fumes from the lighter were making him feel a bit woozy.

"Ah Jack, you're next," Mr Bell said as he stretched up after burning Lina's photograph of an Anderson Shelter.

"But you have already burnt mine," Jack fibbed, holding his work behind his back.

"Are you sure Jack? I don't remember burning yours or Malcolm's letters."

"No, you did Mr Bell," Malcolm lied as he also hid his work behind his back.

"Let me see, please," Mr Bell asked, he wasn't suspicious, he genuinely couldn't remember.

"All done, look," Jack quickly replied while flashing his wee-stain papers.

"Oh, you coloured it too, have we run out of tea?"

"Yes, all finished so we decided to colour it yellow, so it looks like fire damage" Jack lied again while simultaneously kicking over the bowl of tea.

"Oh...okay...great, then I guess we have done here and it's nearly time for assembly," Mr Bell confirmed. He was confused, giddy and in need of his cup of tea, so had no energy to question Jack further.

Jack and Malcolm breathed a huge sigh of relief, not telling the truth had seemed a much better option than being honest, to be honest.

"So, I can see that there are no more questions about Mr Grimshaw, then I think it's time to move on."

Mr X had just spent twenty minutes in assembly in another *some people* session. The usual subjects, but this time there was a strange soggy mess in the boys' toilet, and of course some people had robbed the local bank, disappeared and now were back on the scene. After answering questions about the mystery surrounding Mr Grimshaw, he could see that the children all still had their hands up but he had had enough and decided the best way forward was to pretend that he couldn't see the hands raised in the air.

"Now, exciting news, as part of our Green Week, today we have been joined by a local artist who is going to explain a great way to turn trash into art." Mr X had got slightly frazzled by all the bank robbery talk that he hadn't actually had a chance to meet the artist who was standing to his right. So, he turned to Mr Bell who could see that he needed help. Mr Bell mouthed the artist's name.

"He is called Evan Steven," Mr Bell mouthed in an exaggerated manner.

Mr X nodded, "I would like to introduce you all to Mr Even Stevens." He thought it was a slightly odd name.

"It's Steven," the artist replied.

"I'm so sorry, I would like to introduce you all to Steven Even-Stevens," Mr X proudly announced. The artist was too nice to contradict Mr X again so he just went along with it.

So, Mr Steven Even-Stevens politely went on to explain to the children that they were going to do a beach clean-up that afternoon and any rubbish found would be used to make a huge sculpture in the playground.

The children thought it was a cool idea, as lots of plastic had been washing up on their wonderful beach recently, and they had lots of questions for Mr Steven Even-Stevens. A plan was hatched to let each class take a different part of the beach to tidy, then sort through everything back at school, either recycling items or using them for the sculpture.

During lunchtime, however, the conversation predictably went back to Mr Grimshaw.

"If you robbed a bank, where would you hide the money?" Chloe asked while the kids sat around in the playground.

"No need to hide it, it would be spent in one day," Jack confidently declared.

"I'd bury it for sure," Tim replied. "Maybe on a beach." Suddenly, several children glanced at each other, as if they had unexpectedly solved the case.

"Maybe a beach you knew very well, like this one!" Lucy screamed.

"Yes, but no one saw him here the day of the storm or the day after," Kath interjected putting a dampener on proceedings.

"I did," Fred piped up.

"What! Why didn't you say anything!" the entire class screamed.

"No one asked," Fred replied matter of fact.

"When did you see him?" Kyle barked.

"The next day, I came down here with my mum to see how bad the damage to the school was and I saw Mr Grimshaw and his wife carrying two big sports bags," Fred began feeling the pressure and turned his ahead away from the group.

"Which way, where?" Kyle screamed but Fred was back in his happy place and wouldn't answer.

Ellie again was summoned to elicit an answer from Fred. She put down her book, cleared her throat and winked to the gang. "Who's your favourite member of One Direction?"

"None of them," replied Tim.

"The dead one," replied Oscar.

"The one who wears the top hat and has side-burns," replied Hettie.

"All of them," replied Lola who went into a bit of a trance thinking about them.

Fred heard something to do with directions, "He buried the bag about four hundred metres west of the school, near the trees, approximately a three-minute walk from here."

Mr Bell meanwhile was trying to display the World War Two letters, but he just couldn't figure out why Jack and Malcolm's letters were so different, he was also suspicious they smelt a wee bit different too, so when Dave and Alan entered to ask him about the beach clean-up, he was holding Jack's letter close to his nose and sniffing like a police dog, so he wasn't really paying attention.

"Mr Bell can we clean the area, near the trees?" Alan asked.

"Erm...sure...why?"

"No reason," Dave lied.

So, about half an hour later Mr Steven Even-Stevens had split up the classes and the children all fanned out in opposite directions around the school.

Within seconds Mr Bell's class had made a bee-line for the area Fred had told them about. Mr Bell and the other teachers thought this would be an excellent time to coordinate things from a few rocks that skirted the water's edge, so his class had no prying eyes on their beach clean-up-stroke-treasure-hunt. None of the teachers spotted Mr Bell's class armed with spades that they had sneaked out of the games room.

"Tell us when we are in the right place Fred," Chloe whispered. Fred just carried on walking, then suddenly stopped near a bush that was growing on the fringe of the beach and simply pointed down. Chloe waved like mad to the other children but caught Mr Bell's attention too.

"Hi! Mr Bell, we miss you, you...you enjoy your well-earned cup of tea," Chloe fibbed whilst giving Mr Bell the thumbs up.

Mr Bell thought there were some strange things happening today but then he smiled to himself, although they may be silly sometimes, they are all good, honest, polite kids, so he gave the thumbs up back to Chloe and closed his eyes.

"Get digging, we haven't got long until the old fool comes snooping around," Chloe instructed her class-mates.

The kids dug as if their lives depended on it and it wasn't long before they struck gold, well they struck canvas. Dave and Oscar hurled a multi-coloured sports bag out the ground. It was half opened but disappointingly for the treasure hunters all it contained were clothes. On further inspection, Tim found two passports.

"These are fake, look!" he whispered loudly. The passport had a picture of Mr Grimshaw but the name said Robin Banks.

"Nice touch!" Jack declared.

Mrs Grimshaw's passport had the name Greta Whey-Driver.

"Doesn't work quite as well, but still clever," Jack said dreamily, as if he had just found two new role-models to model his future life upon.

"The bag was open and I can't find any men's underwear anywhere," Chloe announced.

"So?" the kids chorused.

"So that explains why the police found a few of Mr Grimshaw's things near the beach, they must have fallen out in his rush to hide the bag."

"Excellent point Chloe," Ellie said. "If this were a book, then not only would it be a fantastic read, but the plot is beginning to make sense." All the children nodded in agreement, if this were a book, it would probably be award winning.

"Quick, over here, I've found another bag," squealed Kyle, and with the help of one of the twins they dragged up an identical bag, however this time it was all zipped up.

"Wait!" Chloe instructed, she scanned the beach, Mr Bell looked like he was in the land of nod, the other teachers were chatting and

Mr Steven Even-Stevens was a mile down the other way carrying about six bin bags full of plastic.

A hush descended over the children, as Tim was elected to unzip the bag.

"Stone the crows!" screamed Hettie, everyone else was struck dumb, as the unzipping revealed the bag was stuffed full of money. Well it was actually neatly packed with thousand dollars bundles. Only a very low pitched, dramatic fart from Malcolm woke the children from their state of dumbstruckness.

"How much do you think is in there?" Lina finally managed to squeak.

"Fifty-thousand," whispered Fred.

The children didn't even bother questioning how Fred knew, his exclusive revelations were now becoming commonplace, and after a quick count by Tim, the amount was confirmed.

"Fifty thousand dollars," Oscar mouthed.

"Fifty thousand dollars," the twins said in unison.

"Fifty thousand guineas," Hettie confirmed.

"Fifty thousand dollars," Alan mouthed.

"Forty thousand dollars," Jack professed.

"It's fifty, Jack," Kyle corrected.

"Is it though?"

"Erm...yes, it is Jack."

"But is that what we are telling Mr Bell?"

"Pardon?"

"Well I know for a fact the bank's computers were down that day because of the storm, and they have no idea how much was stolen, plus it's insured...so if we were to take a little finder's fee, then what's the harm?"

"That's stealing Jack," Tim replied.

"You can't steal stolen money, it's a well-known fact, look at Robin Hood," Malcolm added helpfully.

"He gave money to the poor, Malcolm," Chloe interjected.

"Exactly, often poor children, like us," Jack replied.

In times of trouble, as usual, all eyes fell on Ellie to show which sensible path should be taken. She put down her book (appropriately she was reading Treasure Island) and addressed the treasure finders. Thoughts of Mr Bell's wonderful words about honesty, morality and trustworthiness were still fresh in her mind as she gave one of the most important speeches of her life.

A few moments later, Tim and Lucy were standing next to Mr Bell and the other teachers on the water's edge, and presenting him with a multi-coloured sports bag.

"Wow, I've just counted it and there's forty thousand dollars in there!" Mr Bell screamed.

"Really, we didn't bother counting it, we thought the honest thing was to come straight here and show you."

"You did the right thing kids and we will take it to Mr X immediately."

"Thirty thousand dollars," Mr X yelled, "oh my goodness Mr Bell, what an honest bunch you are, Mr Dijon the school manager will be here in a minute, I'm sure he will want to know all about it, why don't you get back to the beach clean-up."

A few minutes later Mr Dijon was presented with a bag containing an incredible twenty thousand dollars and he was quick to thank Mr X, the teachers and students for their honest nature.

When the police collected the bag with a whopping ten thousand dollars from Mr Dijon, the whole school was praised for their truthful attitude.

That night Mr Grimshaw and his wife were caught on the beach by the police trying to reconnect with their sports bags.

The next morning it was all over the media and the Grimshaws gave a quick interview on the way to court.

"What did you plan to do with the ten thousand dollars?" a pushy reporter shouted.

"Ten thousand? Ten thousand? We have made some big mistakes, and honestly the biggest was thinking we were stealing a lot more than that. We are really sorry for what we did and to the staff and children of Sandy Primary, we let you down, crime never pays," an exhausted and dishevelled Mr Grimshaw replied.

The children watching on new tablets, the teachers watching on their new televisions, the headmaster watching under his new wig and the school owner watching in his new limousine couldn't agree more. Honestly.

CHAPTER 09

The Author Visit

"Sorry I'm late mate, are ya drinking that tea?"

A young, blonde, muscular man had just walked through the gate, straight up to Mr Bell and snatched his latest cup of tea out of his hand. "I'm not drinking it now, no. So, you must be our author then, come to inspire the children?" Mr Bell replied in annoyed tones.

"That I am mate, pleased to meet ya, the name's Nick Battersby, all the way from Oz, but you can call me Nick," he grabbed Mr Bell's hand and shook it violently. He then took a huge slurp of the tea, "Got any sugar mate?"

Now Mr Bell was a patient man, but he did have some strange quirks. He hated people who were late. He also thought anyone who put sugar in their tea, ideally should be executed, particularly if it was his tea that had just been stolen. He also hated people grabbing his hand, and to be honest wasn't too keen on Australians. The few he had met seemed strong, confident, athletic, good at cricket and could have beaten him in a fight in about ten seconds (and that was just the women). In short, the polar opposite of Mr Bell himself.

"Likewise. I'm Mr Bell but you can call me Mr Bell, a warm welcome to Sandy Primary, and no I don't have any sugar," Mr Bell snarled sarcastically.

"Gees what an impressive sculpture, what the heck is it mate?" Nick asked, whilst still shaking hands and pulling Mr Bell around to face it.

Mr Bell grabbed his hand out of its vice-like grip and faced the recently completed statue that stood by the entrance. "It's an abstract piece showing the destruction to the bottom of the ocean by plastic blown into water by the wind."

WALLY THE WOMBAT
AND HIS HEALTHY FRUIT BASED
ADVENTURES IN THE
UNIVERSE

"It looks like a huge bum mate!" Nick responded quite seriously.

He was right. Mr Steven Even-Steven's statue was impressive, all materials were recycled, mostly plastic and it was a beautiful, meaningful piece. However, from certain angles it did look like a huge bottom. It took Jack ten seconds to nickname it, *Big Plastic Windy Bottom*, and the name had stuck.

After the drama of Mr Grimshaw, the school needed some funds to complete the sculpture. Strangely, thousands and thousands of dollars were donated from the children, teachers, principal and owner. So, the school was able to make a plaque for the sculpture, add some benches to the playground and even buy new games for The Games Room. Nearly forty thousand dollars was collected, a case of guilt had fallen over the school.

There was even a little left to buy a new flag. Mr Grimshaw's pants had been taken away for further forensic examination and Lina who was the most talented artist in the school had designed a new one, two trees and a huge sun shining, with SPS in the foreground.

"Anyway, I'd better crack on," Nick eventually uttered after being mesmerised for several seconds by Mr Steven Even-Stevens' Big Plastic Windy Bottom. "Did you get the stuff I asked for?"

Mr Bell ushered Nick to his classroom, his class and all the other children were already upstairs in the assembly room waiting for the author and handed him a plastic bag. "Yes, there is a selection of fruit – apples, pears, oranges and bananas and a large bacon sandwich with extra ketchup, what's it all for?"

"My book is about healthy living mate, so I invented this amazing game with the fruit, I'm gonna play it later with the kids."

"What's the bacon sandwich for?"

"My breakfast mate, I'm starvin' and between you and me, I can't be bothered with eating fruit, way too healthy! Any more tea going by the way?"

Mr Bell's temple began to throb, he shakily ran his fingers through his hair and took a deep breath. He had been up extra early basically buying Nick his breakfast, the rest Nick had stolen from him. "Didn't you have breakfast at your hotel?" he snarled.

"Hotel? I kipped on the beach, much cheaper. I have been travelling round the world doing this for the last few months, making a fortune mate, the more I save, the longer I can go without going back to the classroom," Nick beamed.

"You're a teacher, and we are actually paying you!" Mr Bell yelped.

"Yep mate, got to see a Mr X for a big, fat cheque later. I used to teach Upper Primary, just like you I reckon, but I hatched a plan to escape from being with a bunch of annoying kids all day. You ain't got a spare sofa I could use tonight, have you?" Nick replied confidently whilst taking an enormous bite out of his bacon butty.

Mr Bell had to restrain himself not to punch this annoying tea stealer on the nose. Not only was he an infuriating cheapskate, he had unlocked the secret that every teacher dreamed of, to actually one day escape from the classroom.

"No sorry, maybe you should sleep under the stars again, heard the forecast is excellent," Mr Bell fibbed, there was another storm due that evening.

"Cheers mate. Do ya want to know the secret of success?" Nick asked whilst letting out a huge burp.

Mr Bell couldn't stand the man standing in front of him, yet weirdly he was intrigued as to how Nick had managed to live the teachers' dream.

"Go on."

"Two tips. Firstly, always write about what you know. Secondly don't let the kids ask any of their own questions. Simple"

"Okay...so the first point, is your book set in a school?" Mr Bell replied intrigued.

"No mate, it's about a space travelling wombat who is looking to stay healthy," Nick replied whilst rubbing his stomach to help digest his hearty breakfast.

"Okay...so are you an expert in the areas of space, health and... er...wombats?" Mr Bell quizzed, pretty confused.

"Well I know that our galaxy has about four planets, wombats are like kangaroos and fruit well important as it keeps your teeth healthy, so yeah, you could say I'm an expert," Nick replied self-assuredly.

Mr Bell stared at the back-packing moron standing in front of him in a state of shock, but instead of challenging Nick's factual knowledge, he decided to continue to listen to his warped wisdom.

"Makes sense," Mr Bell responded sarcastically. "What about the second tip?"

"Ah yes, when you are doing these book tours, don't let the kids ask anything, they are all dumb, most of them aren't even listening."

"Now hold on a minute!"

"Listen mate, it's true, if you let them ask questions, they say stuff like...what's your favourite colour? Do you like potatoes? Or they put their hand up and say something like I read a book once...they never listen, so don't let them ask a question, unless you know what it's going to be, simple!"

Mr Bell couldn't even respond, he was so furious with Nick's comments. He knew the children of Sandy primary were much more intelligent than that. His face had turned a funny colour and his fists were clenched.

"I can see you don't believe me but since I like you mate, I will let your lot ask three questions, but you'll see I'm right. I have some prepared questions, they can ask those too, here," With that Nick handed Mr Bell a stack of laminated question cards. "Right best get going mate, got another school to visit after lunch, don't want to be late."

Mr Bell couldn't believe the cheek and stupidity of this so-called author and he couldn't wait for his clever, reliable bunch of children to prove Nick wrong, so he politely led him up to the Assembly Room.

"So, for the final time, we haven't installed a lift, next to the stairs is a filing cabinet...filing cabinet...not a lift. I don't want to find any more infants locked in there saying the lights are broken. Is that understood?" Mr X had taken an impromptu, *some people session* and it appeared someone (guess who?) had found a new way to terrorise the younger children with his Lift of Doom.

"Ah Mr Bell is here with our special guest, a big round of applause for Nick Nattersby."

"Cheers everyone, it's Battersby but it great to be here," Nick said as he walked in front of the children. Mr Bell had done a quick about turn to get a vital caffeine shot but he was soon sitting at the back of the room, waiting for the children to prove Nick wrong.

"G'day everyone, today I'd like to share with you my amazing new book called *Wally the Wombat and his Healthy Fruit Based Adventures in The Universe*. I'm incredibly successful and incredibly busy, so I don't normally allow you to ask you own questions. But for my great mate Mr Bell, I will allow three questions before we begin," Nick announced whilst giving the thumbs up to Mr Bell.

"Don't let me down gang," Mr Bell muttered to himself.

A swathe of hands went up in the air and Nick pointed at an infant in the front row. Mr Bell could tell immediately from his bright red curly hair, that it was Lucy's younger brother Tom. He had the same hair colour as his sister and Mr Bell had high hopes for a good question, as Tom was known to be a smart cookie.

"What's your favourite colour?" Tom asked.

"Great question mate, I guess I like red," Nick replied whilst winking at Mr Bell. Coincidently, red was the colour Mr Bell's face had just turned.

"Next question," Nick continued and pointed at another infant sitting near the front. Mr Bell strained his neck to see the second volunteer. It was Aenya, who was very bright but had a reputation for her whacky sense of humour. Mr Bell held his breath.

"Do you like potatoes?" Aenya asked whilst twirling her hair.

"Love 'em mate! Do you?"

"Yes, I have a pet one," Aenya replied. Mr Bell smacked his hand on his head in despair.

"Okay, for your final question, let's go for the older kids," Nick announced whilst scanning the kids sitting at the back.

This was the chance, Fred was asleep so any other child would come up with a great, challenging question. Ellie, Tim, even Jack or Malcolm would put Nick on the back foot. Any other child except Bob.

There are always certain children who never listen but have permanently got their hands in the air, even before they know what they are going to say, Bob was just like that. Unbelievably, he was the only one with his hand raised. Ellie was bored already and reading, Tim was dreaming of vouchers, Jack and Malcolm were seeing who could make the rudest noise by blowing on the backs of their hands.

"Yes mate?" said Nick pointing at Bob.

"Oh no," mumbled Mr Bell

"Er, I read a book once," Bob announced proudly whilst nodding and adding nothing else to his comment.

"Fascinating mate, really fascinating," Nick replied mockingly whilst smiling at Mr Bell.

Mr Bell's humiliation was complete. Bizarrely, Nick was right and now his torture would have to continue as Nick indicated to him to hand out the laminated questions that he had prepared earlier. Mr Bell was too annoyed, so he passed the cards to Miss Tree to give to the children.

Miss Tree handed the first card to one of the twins. "Are you a brilliant author?" he or she read.

"Yes I am. Next question."

Miss Tree handed one to Oscar, who wanted to ask about how many, if any, of the characters died in the book but was forced to ask whether Nick had always been so talented.

"I guess I was just born lucky," Nick replied.

"What inspires you?" Tim read from the next card.

"I don't write books for the money mate. I am making loads, and loads and loads of cash by the way but that's not the point. It's not to escape the classroom either. I love teaching and kids, honestly," Nick winked at Mr Bell who now needed a doctor. "I do it to inspire children, if just one poor child in Africa gets inspired by one of my books, then my job is done." Nick then pretended to wipe a tear from his eyes, whilst glancing at Mr Bell and making a gesture with his fingers as if he were counting cash.

"What are your favourite books?" Kyle was forced to ask.

"I love the one about the boy witch and the other one about the boy who goes to the chocolate warehouse. Charlie Potter and Harry and the Chocolate Warehouse, I think they are called."

Mr Bell started laughing, he realised Nick truly didn't have a clue. Miss Tree handed out the next question.

"Why do you like those books?" Lola sang.

"I want my books to be the same, these great books made loads of money...er...I mean they make loads of children happy," Nick explained sincerely.

"Can you read some of your book to us?" Alan asked.

"No, sorry I am way too busy, you'll have to buy a copy!" Nick answered cheerfully.

Immediately, all the kids started booing, they had looked forward to listening to a real author read their work so this was a big disappointment. From somewhere in the room a chant of "Read it, Read it," sprang up. The chant weirdly seemed to begin at the back of the room where Mr Bell was sitting. It also initially sounded a bit like "Read it you lazy idiot," but that couldn't have been true.

Soon the whole assembly room was in unison. "Read it, read it, read it, twenty six, read it, read it!" they chanted. Mr Bell moved to the front of the room, and from behind it looked like he was trying to calm the children down, but actually he was acting like a conductor and encouraging them to shout louder.

Nick gulped, the assembled hoard looked pretty wild and he realised his only way out alive was to read some of his book.

As all this had been going on, Miss Andrews had been tottering in, trying her best to disturb proceedings whilst carrying several boxes of Nick's books which he had sent to school earlier. Mr Bell dashed over to grab one and cheerfully presented it to Nick.

Nick hesitantly opened it, "Okay, I will read the first couple of pages."

Mr Bell was convinced either Nick couldn't actually read, or more likely if he read the book and it was claptrap, no one would want to buy it.

Nick cleared his throat and read, "Mum, my teeth are falling out," said Wally the Wombat.

"You need some fruit Wally, why don't you use your strong kangaroo-like legs to jump to the nearest planet to Earth, Jupiter and get some."

So, Wally the Wombat jumped and went past the Sun which is a big hot Planet and the moon which is another planet made of cheese and landed on tiny Jupiter. He saw some apples growing in the ground, because that's where apples grow and ate some. Apple juice is like toothpaste and suddenly Wally's teeth were all clean. To make them shine more Wally needed to jump through a black hole to the twin planets of Pluto and Goofy to collect bananas.

Nick stopped and looked up.

Silence. Absolute silence.

Nick could just about read, but the book was absolutely out of this world in terms of rubbishness. The children just glanced at each other confused and Mr Bell had nearly wet himself laughing. He was convinced none of the Sandy Primary kids would be ordering any copies, and Nick would have his extended round-the-world vacation cut short.

"Anyway, if you want to know what happened to Wally or want to learn some more space facts, you will have to buy the book!" Nick stammered, he was on the back foot but he still had a couple of tricks up his sleeve to win over the audience.

"Right who wants to play a game?"

All the hands shot up, Nick knew how to get the kids back on side, Primary kids love games and Nick knew that well.

"You, come up mate," he said pointing at Jack. Jack made his way to the front. "Now Wally was an expert in sniffing out fruit, let's see if you are. I'm gonna hold a piece of fruit in my hand, close your eyes and smell it, if you guess it right, you get to keep it mate."

"Cool," replied Jack and he shut his eyes. Nick held a banana in his hand in front of Jack's nose.

"Bacon. It smells of bacon, is bacon a fruit?" Nick quickly put the banana in his other hand. "Or banana. It smells of banana. Is banana a fruit?"

"Yes, it is, here, keep the banana!"

"Have you got any bacon?"

"No mate, now get off, next up is..." Nick continued pointing at Lucy.

Lucy successfully sniffed out a pear, and the game went on. The kids loved it and Nick had his swagger back. After Kyle had won a banana, Nick announced, "Okay gang, got to go soon but if anyone wants to order my book, make a line, I will sign them and you also get a free piece of fruit with every order!"

The kids went wild, the thought of something for nothing and they had soon forgotten how bad his book was and were filling out order forms and scrambling for the free fruit that Mr Bell had bought earlier that day.

"Unbelievable," Mr Bell muttered to himself. Nick had still managed to turn this disaster into a profit as much as he couldn't stand Nick, he had to admire his cheek.

About twenty minutes later, with tonnes of books ordered and the fruit all gone, Nick was ready to leave. "I'll be off then mate, thanks for letting me inspire your kids today."

"Not sure inspire is the right word, I was thinking more like confuse, but you've inspired me, maybe I will write a book, if you can do it, surely anyone can," Mr Bell replied mockingly.

"You write a book! Mate not a chance, not sure you are ready to leave the classroom Mr Bell, you gotta be born with the talent and a gift for words like what I got, stick to the day job!" Nick chortled loudly. "Beside mate, what on earth have you got to write about?" With that Nick slapped Mr Bell on the back and strolled out of the school.

Mr Bell was going to make some sarcastic comment about Nick's book or having a safe journey but then he paused. Nick was right. To write a book you needed an inspiring setting, Mr Bell looked around the tumble-down school on the amazing beach and he rubbed his chin and thought.

You would also need larger than life characters, he glanced at Mr X striding across the playground to talk to Jack and Malcolm about putting their banana peels right outside the staffroom door. Miss Andrews holding her back as she had just coincidently slipped on a banana skin. He then noticed Ellie with her head in a book, Tim trying to break into the Games Room, Kyle talking about him mum, the twins, Bob and Dave trying to tidy up Dave's desk, Fred still asleep and Hettie playing marbles. Then his mind turned to Mr Grimshaw and Miss James, even their doctor, Doctor Hoo. He rubbed his chin again and thought some more.

But what stories could you actually write? In this simple little school, everything was completely normal. Well...apart from the owner, principal, teachers, children, school bus, ability to raise money, run a fair or a Sports Day. The over use of idioms was also a bit bonkers as was the clambering to enter a Games Room with no games in it. It wasn't as if the school was rebuilt by the children after a huge hurricane and for several months had a pair of underpants up the flagpole. And to have a bank-robbing teacher on their staff, or a statue of an artist's huge plastic windy bottom in the middle of the playground, was all completely normal and boring. Mr Bell almost drew blood rubbing his chin again.

That evening, Mr Bell couldn't eat, he couldn't sleep, and he had a huge plaster on his chin that was really annoying him. So, at about three in the morning, he got out of bed, made a bucket full of tea, grabbed a pen and notepad and was poised to write. But where could his story begin? Suddenly it all made sense and he wrote... CHAPTER 1: THE REBUILD.

CHAPTER 10

HETTIE

An aptronym is a word that describes someone's name that is suited to who they are. Occasionally a perfect fit occurs. For example, the footballer Michael Ball or the weather lady called Sara Blizzard. Steph O'Scope the doctor or Pablo Paintbrush, the artist (a couple of those are actually true). So when Hettie Victoria Mary Poppins Tiny Tim Florence Nightingale Dickens was born, there was a good chance she would be an example of an aptronym.

Hettie's father was the last chimney sweep in the land and her mother sold breadcrumbs to feed the birds (tuppence a bag). Her best friend was her cousin called Cleopatra Pyramid Pharoah Slave Hieroglyphics Nile Ra Sphinx (who was brought up by her mummy). Cleo was obsessed by all things from ancient Greece. As mentioned, only occasionally does a perfect fit happen.

Here is a list of Hettie-isms from the story:

Cor blimey govna—wow!

Stone the crows—oh dear!

Gas-pipes—trousers

Afternoonified—smart

Bang up to the elephant—perfect

Batty-fanged—to beat up

Guinea-coin worth twenty-one shillings

Hettie hopes you found this book nanty narking!

CPSIA information can be obtained
at www.ICGtesting.com
Printed in the USA
LVHW080030230419
615090LV00007B/362/P